W9-BXW-606

Five
Days
Apart

Five
Days
Apart

A Novel

Chris Binchy

HARPER

An Imprint of HarperCollinsPublishers
www.harpercollins.com

HarperCollins books may be purchased for educational, business, or sales promotional use. For information, please write: Special Markets Department, HarperCollins Publishers, 10 East 53rd Street, New York, NY 10022.

FIRST EDITION

Designed by Renato Stanisic

Library of Congress Cataloging-in-Publication Data
Binchy, Chris.
Five days apart : a novel / Chris Binchy. — 1st ed.
p. cm.
ISBN 978-0-06-170435-2
1. Young men—Fiction. 2. Dating (Social customs)—Fiction. 3. Ireland—Fiction. I. Title.
PR6102.I5F58 2010
823'.92—dc22
2009040575

10 11 12 13 14   ID/RRD   10 9 8 7 6 5 4 3 2 1

FOR SIOBHAN, MICHAEL, AND MARIANNE

I saw her first. I was in the kitchen getting ice when she arrived. Three of them came together, all girls, and I could see them in the hall. They were apologizing for being late and taking off their coats, one of them introducing the others to the host, Paul. It was all confusion, everybody talking and nobody listening, and then they came into the kitchen to get a drink. Paul was trying to sort them out, but he was already drunk, stumbling around the place, and he couldn't find glasses or wine or an opener. Picking up empty bottles and shaking them, saying there definitely was more, I know I had more, and looking in the fridge, then closing it and opening it again as if something might have changed, as if it might have replenished itself.

I was leaning against the sink at the edge of the whole exchange. I was smiling, trying not to laugh at him. I looked away, and when I turned back there she was, smiling right back at me. I hadn't noticed her until then. They were all one noisy entity when they arrived. But I was looking at her now, straight into her eyes, and it felt like something.

"Oh," I said out loud.

The other girls stopped talking for a second and looked at me. I turned to the ground and the conversation resumed. When I looked up again, she was still watching me. I could feel my mouth curl, the way it does when I don't know, when I'm not sure. She smiled and then Paul said that there was drink in the living room and they were gone. I stood there buzzing, a charge in my stomach and in my hands, which shook a little as I drank. I had to go after her. I couldn't let it end there. But she was with other people and what was I supposed to do? Go up and say, "Hi, I'm David, I couldn't help noticing you, you're very beautiful"? "You're a great-looking lady"? "I think we had a real connection"? I'm not an idiot. I know my limits.

So I stayed standing at the counter and drank and tried to work it out. Get Alex, I thought. He'll know what to do. That was exactly how it was. I thought he would help.

He was out in the conservatory with some guys I didn't know from his college.

"Hey," he said when he saw me.

"Hi," I said.

"This is David," he said to the others. "We were in school." They kind of nodded up at me and one of them said hello, as if that was funny in itself. "Hello."

"Do you want some of this?" Alex asked, waving a joint at me vaguely, knowing I wouldn't.

"No," I said. "Can you come in here for a second?"

"Yeah, sure," he said. I went back into the kitchen, and he followed me.

"What's up?"

"There's a girl that just arrived. I don't know. Just. Amazing."

"Where is she?"

"In the living room, I think. Seriously though. Wait till you see."

"Let's go." He was turning away from me. I pulled him back.

"Hang on a second."

"What?"

"Well, I don't want to go in there like a pair of idiots. You're not to be talking shit and acting the lad."

"Who, me?"

"Just don't."

He smiled at me. He was happy and relaxed, at his most dangerous.

"I will be charm itself."

"Okay," I said. "Don't embarrass me."

It was a double room with an open partition in the middle. The heat and smoke and noise hit us as we walked in. A load of people were dancing in the middle, and others were sitting in groups on the floor around the edges and on couches that had been pushed back. The music was so loud it was distorting, the bass pulsing beneath my feet and in my chest.

"That's her," I said to Alex, leaning in to shout in his ear.

"What? Where? Which one?"

"Over there. I'm not going to point, for fuck's sake."

"So nod." I nodded in her direction.

"Oh yeah, okay," he said. "I see her now."

She was sitting on a couch, talking to one of the girls that she had arrived with. Alex didn't say anything else, just walked straight over and sat down beside her. I stood for a second, watching him, and I knew I had to do the same. He was shaking her hand when I arrived, up and down, messing around. She was smiling at him, but I could see she was uncertain.

"This is David," he said, pointing at me. "David, this is . . . ," and he said her name. I didn't hear it but I couldn't ask again, the wrong first impression to give, shouting "What?" like some old fellow, so I just smiled.

"Hi," she said. Her eyes flashed up at me. Just a quick glance to check, then she looked back at Alex and said something that I couldn't make out. The music was too loud. He was sitting beside her, and I was standing at his shoulder as if I was his butler. Her friend was on the far side of the couch, staring across the room at nothing. She seemed bored already. I smiled over at her, but she didn't see me. I went and sat beside her anyway and said hello. She was all right looking.

"How do you know Paul?" I asked her.

"I don't," she said.

Behind her I was watching Alex talk to my girl. He was doing his usual thing, all chat and a little too close. I couldn't see her face but tried to work out from the way she was sitting what she thought of him. It was impossible. As I watched, Alex caught my eye just for a second. He didn't look over, didn't stop talking, but he winked. I couldn't stop myself from grinning back at him.

"What?" the friend asked.

"Sorry?" I said, looking back at her.

"What's funny?"

"Nothing," I said. "Just laughing, you know. So what do you do?" I asked after a minute.

"I'm in college."

"Oh, yeah? What are you studying?"

"Not a whole lot."

I smiled even though it wasn't funny and the way she'd said it didn't make it sound like a joke.

"I mean, what course are you on?"

"Sociology."

"Great," I said. "Interesting."

"Not very."

"I'm doing computer science," I said because, really, she deserved it.

"Oh, yeah?" she said, yawning as she spoke.

"Are you tired?" I asked, but she didn't answer.

So I sat beside her, and we didn't talk. Every so often I would look over at Alex, who seemed to be having a great time. After a few minutes I stood up.

"I'm going to the kitchen," I said to the friend. "Can I get you anything?"

"Like what?"

"I don't know. A beer or something."

"No," she said. "I don't drink beer."

"Okay, so." I tapped Alex on the shoulder. He looked up at me. "Here, do you want a drink?"

"I don't know. Do you want something?" he asked my one. She spoke to me.

"Can I get some wine? White wine?"

"I'll have the same," Alex said, and I wandered off.

When I came back in carrying their drinks, there was nobody on the couch. I looked around and saw the two of them on the far side of the room, dancing beside each other. I went over and handed a drink to her.

"I'll be back in a second," Alex said, and he disappeared. I was left standing with her. I drank from the glass that I had brought for him. She smiled at me and said something.

"Sorry?" I said.

She leaned forward and spoke into my ear.

"Are you in college with Alex?" she asked me. She was so close I could feel her breath against my ear when she spoke. I could smell her perfume, light and grassy.

"No. I was in school with him. We're old friends," I said.

"Okay."

I felt the urge to touch her face or hug her or take her hand and lead her out the door, to make some sort of physical contact with her, but resisted it. I tried to keep it simple for myself.

"I saw you when you arrived," I said. It sounded creepier than I had anticipated.

"I saw you too," she said after a second. "You were in the kitchen, looking nervous."

"Did I look nervous?"

"Very." She was staring at me as she spoke. I tried to hold her gaze, but it was too much.

"I thought I was . . . ," and couldn't think of a word to end the sentence. "The state of Paul," I said instead.

"Is he always like that?"

"Yeah, mostly," I said. "Do you not know him?"

"No."

"He's an arsehole."

"That's not very nice. About your host."

"No, really. It's true."

"Nice house, though."

"Yeah, it's his parents' place."

"Right."

"They're arseholes too."

She laughed at that, and I relaxed a bit. This isn't so bad, I thought to myself. I might get to the end of this conversation without choking to death. Then Alex arrived back.

"Is that mine?" he asked, pointing at the glass I was holding.

"Oh, yeah," I said. He took it, knocked it back, then grabbed her hand.

"Let's dance," he said. She kind of laughed, half resisting but not really.

"Come on," he said turning to me. "Dance with us." They bounced off, him dragging her into the thick of the crowd. I stood there and watched them go. For a moment I thought about it. I thought I could follow and jump up and down with them and pretend to be enjoying myself. But why pretend? He knew I wouldn't want to dance, to watch him make a move on her. There was no point in my hanging around.

I went out into the hall and got my coat. I opened the front door and stood at the top of the steps. It was a freezing still night, the stars shining above. The grass in the park in front of the house was white and sparkly with frost. It smelled like it might snow. I thought about walking home. Let the cold clear my head. I could be in bed in twenty minutes, warm and comfortable and reading a book. This wouldn't seem so bad then. But I knew that when I turned out the light, it would come back. What would have happened? What had I missed? What had she said? What had he done? Once I started to think about it, it would grow until there was nothing else, and I wouldn't be able to sleep. That was what I was like. It was stupid, but I couldn't seem to get beyond it.

I walked down the steps, but at the bottom I stopped and turned around. I went back up and in. I wanted to thank Paul for the party. That's all I was thinking, or that's what I told myself. Say good-bye to him at least. I found him in the main room on the floor, talking with some girl. I didn't see the others.

"I'm going to head," I said to him.

"Okay?" Paul said. He shrugged. "Thanks for coming or whatever."

"It was great," I said.

"Can't have been that great if you're going," he said, and the girl laughed. I didn't look at her.

"I've to be up in the morning," I said.

"On a Sunday?"

"Yes." I was going to give him a reason and then realized that he didn't care. "Yes," I said again.

"Fair enough," he said. "Take it easy."

"See you."

I didn't look into the main room as I left. I'm sure I wanted to, but I didn't. As I was at the door again, Alex came out into the hall and called after me.

"Are you off?"

I didn't say anything or turn to face him. I opened the door.

"Hey." He was standing right behind me now and put his hand on my arm. "Hey."

"What?" I said.

"What's wrong? Why are you going?"

I just looked at him. I remember thinking that he must have known, but it didn't show. He seemed genuine.

"You don't know what's wrong?" I said. "You seriously don't know?"

"No. What is it? Did I do something to piss you off?"

"No," I said. "Or yes, maybe."

"What? Tell me."

I breathed in deep, trying to calm myself.

"That girl," I said.

"What about her?"

"What did you think I was doing? Why did you think I went and got you?"

"So we could go and talk to them? I don't know."

"Them? It wasn't them. It was her. She was the reason."

"You like her?" he asked, as if there was some doubt.

"Yes. Jesus, yes. What did you think?"

"Then why did you get me? Why didn't you go and talk to her yourself?"

"Oh, come on."

"What?"

It seemed unreasonable of him to make me say it.

"I'm no good at that kind of thing. Okay? You know that. You know me."

"So, what was it? You wanted me to introduce you to her?"

"Yes. I don't know. Something like that. I didn't want you to just go and start chatting her up. What did you think? That I'd found a nice girl for you?"

He looked confused, trying to work it out.

"I don't know what I thought. I'm sorry. I wasn't doing anything. I was just being friendly. I mean, I was nice to her. I took her up to dance. I thought you'd join us."

"When did I ever dance?"

"I've seen you dancing."

"With you and a girl? When has that ever happened?"

"Well, I had no idea I was upsetting you. I didn't know you liked her."

"I told you."

"No. You said there was some fucking great-looking girl had just arrived."

"That's not what I said."

"Well, what did you say? It was something like that."

I couldn't remember. It wasn't what I had said that was important. It was what I had meant, but he hadn't understood me. I tried to relax, breathed in slowly before speaking.

"When she arrived, I saw her, and there was something between us. There was a look. I don't know what it was, but I've never had that before. I'm serious. I can't tell you what it was like."

"You didn't tell me that. You didn't tell me anything. I'm sorry if I've pissed you off, but I didn't know about it." He smiled at me, almost shyly, not sure what I would do. "I'm not psychic," he said.

I could feel the tension fading away.

"I thought you'd know me well enough."

"Isn't it good that there are still some things I don't know," he said. He pulled me by the arm back across the hall. "Come on. We'll go back in and you can stroke her hair and tell her how you feel or whatever it is you want to do. I'll stay out of the way."

"Oh, piss off," I said.

But as we were going back in, she was on her way out with her quiet friend.

"There you are," Alex said. "We were just coming to find you."

"We're going to go."

"Now? Why?"

"Fiona has to be up in the morning."

"But you could stay," I said.

She smiled at me.

"No. We'll get a taxi together." Her friend had walked off at this stage without saying anything. "It was good to meet you," she said. They were going. They were nearly gone.

"Can we get your number?" Alex said. "Maybe give you a call and meet up again sometime." She stood and looked at him, waited for a moment.

"Okay," she said.

"It'll be fun," he said. "I promise you. He's normally very entertaining. Just not on top form tonight."

"Too tired," I said.

"Right." She wrote her number on a cigarette box that Alex gave her. He looked at the number when she handed it back to him.

"We'll call you," he said. "We will call you."

"Okay," she said. "Bye." She gave a little wave and walked off.

"See you," I said after her.

"Was that okay?" Alex asked me when she was gone.

"That was why I got you. See, I wouldn't have asked for her number. I thought it might be useful."

I laughed with happiness and some sort of relief.

"I don't think my life will be really happy unless I end up with this girl."

"Oh, Jesus," he said. "Don't say things like that. Let's just get a drink."

So we went into the kitchen to see what there was left in the fridge.

"Are you still here?" Paul asked when he saw me.

"I'm back," I said. "My morning thing was canceled."

"That's great," he said. He was a sarcastic prick, but I didn't care. I wasn't worried about anything. I was going to make this happen.

"What's her name?" I asked Alex as he handed me a glass with something orange in it.

"Camille," he said, and in my head I said it over and over as we drank through until the morning.

CHAPTER TWO

S he never faded from my memory. The next time I saw her she was exactly as I remembered. Her eyes before everything else. A darkness that pulled me in. A rawness in the way she looked at me, as if she recognized something that she couldn't identify for certain. Something that marked me out from everyone else, as if the two of us were some distinct breed. Her skin was pale, and her hair was black. When she smiled, she showed her teeth. Dark hair and pale skin and dark eyes and white teeth. I knew it all after our first meeting. The angles of her cheekbones, her tiny ears, the small birthmark on the right side of her chin, her mouth, the skin at the top of her neck behind her ear. In the weeks and months that followed I spent a lot of time away from her, but no matter how long it had been I could always picture her.

She was my height, tall for a girl. One time early on when we were in a café, she looked up at me standing beside the

table, her head held at an angle, and then without saying anything she got up and stood in front of me, so close that our
noses were almost touching. She put her hand on her head and
then on mine.

"Five foot nine," she said.

"And a half," I said, trying not to blush.

"If you say so," and she walked off without looking back. I
watched her as she went, holding on to the table to stop myself
from collapsing.

Her legs. Her arms. Her arse. Her tits. To see her in a
white T-shirt and linen trousers on a summer evening out the
back of somebody's house, smiling that wide smile that made
me forget everything else, even when it wasn't for me. You
couldn't help but love her. You would have to understand what
it was about her that I saw that first night.

I got Alex to make the call. It seemed better that he do it,
since he was the one who had asked for her number.

"This is all wrong," he told me before he dialed. "She's
going to think I'm the one after her."

"No, she won't. Tell her that we were wondering if she'd
like to meet up."

"Just her and us? That'll scare her."

"Maybe with her friend."

"What was the friend's name?"

"I don't remember."

"This is the one you said was a pain in the arse."

"She wasn't that bad. You might like her."

He sighed.

"Why can't you do it?"

"Because I can't. I'll get all confused and make a mess of it. It's better if you do it. But make it sound casual."

"Casual?"

"Yeah, like it's all very relaxed. Just getting together for a few drinks or whatever."

"So we want to meet them, but if they don't want to do it we don't care?"

"Yeah."

"That's fucking stupid," he said, shaking his head but dialing the number. "Straight to message." He hung up and threw the phone back to me. "I've done my bit. If you want to arrange something, you're going to have to do the work yourself." I looked at him to see if he was joking. "Seriously. If you like this girl, then you make the call."

"But you were going to do it. You knew what to say. You're better at this stuff than I am."

"Well, you're going to have to get over that." He stood up and stretched. "I'll go with you and do whatever you want, but you need to take a bit of initiative."

"Initiative?"

"Yeah."

"Initiative," I said again, trying to work out if I'd ever heard him say the word before.

That was the end of the conversation. For the next few days I kept meaning to do it, but every time I dialed the number, I imagined some horrible scenario—she wouldn't know who I was and I'd have to explain that I was the friend of that guy she'd met at a party, or she'd tell me she had a boyfriend, or she just wouldn't be interested in meeting—and I'd wind up lying on the floor with my head in my hands. I waited for Alex to raise the subject again, but he wouldn't, knowing that I'd plead and beg and that eventually he'd capitulate. This unspoken battle of wills continued for another couple of days. And then one morning, still in bed, I picked up the phone and did it without thinking. Her phone rang. Before I had time to panic, she answered.

"Hello. This is David," I said. "We met you at that party in Paul's house last week. Me and Alex."

"Oh yeah, hi."

"You remember."

"I remember."

"Great. Did I wake you?"

"No. Well. Kind of. Yeah." She laughed, low and growly. I pictured her in bed. "Hello?" she said.

"Sorry," I said. "If it's too early I can call you back."

"No, it's fine. I should be getting up anyway."

"I've been up for hours," I said for no reason. It wasn't even true.

"Good for you," she said.

"I was wondering . . ."

"Yes."

"Would you and your friend like to meet up with us some time? Just for a drink or something?"

"Which friend is that?" she said. "Fiona?"

"Yes. Fiona."

"When are you talking about?"

"I don't know. This weekend, maybe? Saturday?"

"Let me check. I'll give her a call and get back to you, is that all right?"

"Sure. Great, yeah."

"Ten minutes, okay?"

I lay there in bed staring at the ceiling, happy to have made the call but realizing now that this was just the first of several stages I would have to go through if I was ever going to get any closer to her. The prospect was exhausting. The phone rang in my hand.

"Yeah, that's fine. She's on for it."

"Brilliant," I said. "That's great."

"Where do you want to meet?"

I gave her the name of a place near my flat, and we made the arrangement.

"See you then," she said at the end.

I rang Alex straight away.

"Are you free on Saturday to meet Camille and her friend?"

"You rang her?"

"I did."

"Good man. My God. You phoned a girl."

"Don't patronize me. You abandoned me. What else could I do after? Are you on for it?"

"Sure."

"The friend's name is Fiona, by the way."

"Is she really awful?"

"She's fine when you get to know her," I said. "Full of chat."

When the day came, I cleaned the flat. I changed the bedclothes, tidied my room, opened the windows, took the rubbish downstairs. I bought wine and coffee and food and tried to make the living room look all right. I wanted to give the impression of somebody tasteful but not too uptight. I spent hours trying to get it right.

I talked to Alex, and we arranged to meet at a quarter to nine so that we'd both be there when they arrived, but he got delayed or something. It meant that I was standing on my own at the bar when she came in. People noticed her. She looked beautiful, completely wrong for me. I was out of my depth and could feel my throat tightening. She smiled when she saw me.

"Hi," she said. "The others not here yet?"

"No," I said. "I'm sure they'll be along soon. Traffic or whatever."

She leaned in to kiss me, and I put a hand on her arm, then took it away again as if I was afraid to touch her. I knew it was going to be awkward before it happened.

"You look well," she said.

"Thanks." I looked around for the fucking barman, but there was no sign of him. "So do you," I said, five seconds too late.

It wasn't easy. I was worried that she might think that I'd arranged it so that it would just be the two of us, alone together. I heard myself say twice that I didn't know where Alex was and then had to stop myself from saying it again. She was picking up on my nervousness, standing a step too far away from me as I tried to order. When Fiona arrived, it was a relief. I greeted her like an old friend.

"Have you been here long?" she asked Camille.

"Five minutes."

"Not even that," I said.

Then Alex arrived, and the tension faded away. Without him it would have been a very short evening. They all went and found a table while I stood at the bar to order. He came up after a minute.

"Sorry," he said. "Were you all right?"

"I was fine."

"Shit. I don't know what happened. The day just disappeared on me."

"Stop apologizing. Don't worry about it."

I stood, trying to get the barman's attention.

"Are you all right?" Alex asked me. I tried to smile. I could feel my heart thumping.

"I am fine."

"You seem a bit wound up."

"Yeah, well you know." He nodded.

"Nervous?" he said after a second. "About her?"

"Her," I said. "That's it exactly."

He looked across at the two of them sitting at the table.

"She is a fine thing, all right. I mean, the friend's not bad, but Jesus, your one is something else." I was staring at him when he turned back. "What?"

"That's not helping."

He shrugged.

"Why?" he said. "I was just saying that you've got good taste."

"That's not what you were saying. At all." I tried to relax, but it wasn't easy. The barman seemed incapable of seeing me. "Is there something wrong with this fellow? Has he had a stroke or something? Hello?" I called, waving.

"Hello," he said, waving back but not moving. Smart fellow.

"Can you serve me?" I called. He came over and stood in front of me for a second without saying anything. I ordered, and he nodded his head back.

"Calm down," Alex said when he'd gone. "It would not be good to get thrown out right now."

"I'm calm," I said. "It's just this fucking guy."

I wasn't calm. It was doubt. Worry. The distance between how I had hoped tonight would be and how it was turning out. I could have left. It seemed like a good idea at that moment. To just walk out without saying anything. Easier. But no. I was being stupid. She was probably nervous herself. I looked over and saw the two girls laughing. They were happy. We were all there now. The barman was putting the drinks down in front of me. I handed him the money, and he took it without speaking.

"I think I've upset him," I said to Alex.

It was better after that. I talked to Fiona, or I asked her questions and she talked. She'd got over whatever had been eating her that night at the party and talked like she'd just been let out after twenty years in solitary. I didn't know what the difference was. Camille was sitting beside me, facing the other way as she talked to Alex. I could feel the warmth of her body, her thigh touching off mine when she sat forward to lift her drink from the table. I could feel it but not see it as I looked Fiona in the eye and smiled and nodded and lost track of what she was saying over and over again. When it was Camille's turn to go to the bar, she touched me on the arm.

"What do you want?" she said when I turned.

"What do I want?" I said, trying to be flirty but sounding thick.

"To drink?" she said, almost smiling.

"Oh. Right. The same," I said.

I drank slowly, half finishing pints and then pushing them away when a new one came. Fiona was getting drunk, and her stories started to ramble. I could feel Camille pressing against me, almost leaning back on me now, and I hoped she was drunk too. I didn't move.

When they stopped serving, we talked about where to go. There were names of places in town mentioned, but we couldn't agree. Too many options, and nobody willing to make a decision.

"We could go back to my place if you want," I said. "It's five minutes from here."

"Okay," Fiona said.

"If you're sure?" Camille said.

"Do you have drink?" Alex asked.

"I think there's some wine," I said. There were three bottles in the fridge. Waiting. I knew where the opener was.

We put on our coats and they got their stuff together.

"Good night," I shouted at the barman. He lifted his head and didn't say anything. Alex and I laughed.

"What's that about?" Fiona asked me as we were going down the stairs.

"He's a lovely fellow," I said. "We're regulars."

Then it was me and her standing on the street.

"What happened to the others?" I asked when I realized.

"I don't know," she said. "Maybe gone to the bathroom or something."

"Both of them?" I opened the door and looked up. There was no sign. "Hang on there a second," I said to Fiona and ran back up the stairs.

At the top as I turned into the landing, I saw the two of them wrapped around each other. She had one hand on the back of his head and her other arm around his waist. For a second I didn't realize what was happening, thought instead that maybe he'd been helping her put on her coat and they'd got entangled or something. I didn't say anything, but they must have heard me as I arrived. They broke apart, and she smiled at me over his shoulder, a little embarrassed maybe but nothing more than that. Alex turned and saw me.

"David," he said. "We were just coming." I left, ran back down the stairs, almost falling on the way, steadying myself against the paneled wall and then out onto the street again.

"Are we going?" Fiona asked when I got outside. I stopped and looked at her.

"What is it?" she said, and she took a step closer and touched my face. "What are they up to?" It was obvious now.

"Nothing," I said, pushing her hand away. "Look, I'm not feeling great. I'm going to go. I'm sorry, but maybe another time."

I crossed the road without looking back and turned a corner, then ran home from there. In the flat, panting, I opened one of the bottles, poured myself a glass, and flopped onto the couch. I drank it quickly, then poured another. The room mocked me, its order and cleanliness all wrong for me here alone. I threw an ashtray across the room and pushed a pile of papers off the coffee table onto the floor. It was idiotic. Was the passionate gesture supposed to impress myself? I went over and picked up the pieces of broken glass, then put them in the bin. I was sweating, still breathing fast after the run. I tried to think in short sentences. It was a stupid idea. This kind of thing would never happen for me. Had he known all along that this was where it was heading? Had she? Had I? I could blame both of them, or I could blame my own stupid self for believing a fantasy. Neither scenario would make me feel any better.

I thought he would come over. That guilt or worry might bring him to the door. That he might want to tell me how it had happened in a way that would make it seem not so bad. He knew that I wanted her, what I was trying to do, and still he couldn't stop himself. I closed my eyes and slapped the side of my head when I thought of how much I had told him. Had he even heard me, or had he been thinking all along about how he was going to get her? Like I had sat beside Fiona tonight, smiling at her and nodding and thinking how badly I wanted to be with her friend. I sat on the couch and drank and waited for the doorbell to tell me what was going to happen next. I woke there the following morning, sick and stiff and hungover.

CHAPTER THREE

I've lived a life of building significance into the smallest everyday interactions with women. Smiles in shops. A coincidentally turning head. Eyes meeting in a mirror or in a car stuck in traffic. The hand brushing off mine on a swaying crowded train. Somebody walking beside me, turning into the same street. These incidents were the starting point for my fantasies. Over and over I went through the same process, imagining what could have been. I would return to these happy scenarios later as if they were memories, replaying the specific events even when the original girl's features had become hazy.

At fourteen in Irish college I sat on a beach with a girl that I liked, both of us waiting for me to do something, and eventually when I couldn't think of what that was, I asked her where her parents were.

"The Isle of Man," she said looking away.

"Do they live there?" I asked her then.

"No," she said. "Just a holiday."

I spent a year visualizing a world where I'd kissed her instead of killing the moment by speaking. It would have been easier to do it right. The bloody Isle of Man.

There was a French teacher in school when I was sixteen whose voice sounded different when she spoke to me. Softer, warmer, less French. Alex noticed it too. On a school trip in a hotel in Madrid I went to her room at ten o'clock at night to ask her could I use the phone in my bedroom. She opened her hotel room door in a bra and tracksuit bottoms. I don't know what she was thinking. I could have been anyone. I looked at the ground and forgot what I was there for, apologized, walked away. I never told Alex about it, but I thought about it for months afterward, trying to work out if she knew it was me on the other side of the door. If I'd got the question out, would something different have happened? Would she have reached out to me, told me to come in, closed the door behind me? Maybe. It was almost enough.

There was a girl I passed every day at the same time on her way to work in a travel agency across from the college who never looked at me, but she knew I was there. The same little flick of her head away from me. Every day walking past her on an empty street and I never acknowledged her, because if I did, who knew what might happen?

How many others? Beautiful girls or girls that only I seemed to notice. Girls who nearly and almost and might just have. But never did. I never said. I never stopped and asked or told. It might have worked out if I had. I could have been transformed, might have seen something in one of their faces that made me relax and realize that they were as keen as I was. I could have come up with the first line, something funny to defuse the situation, and after that it would be easy. I knew it should be easy. But the fact that I never did anything shows how unrealistic I thought it was that I would get it right.

The first time I kissed a girl was when I was seventeen. I was drunk at a party in the house of some friend of Alex's and it had nothing to do with me. I was sitting on a couch trying to keep the room from taking off, and a girl sat beside me. She didn't say anything, just leaned over and kissed me. She pushed me back and lay on top of me and we just kept at it. I didn't know her name or what she looked like. I didn't care. I was just glad that at last it was happening and tried to silence the weedy little voices talking about me that might have been in my head.

That was like a breakthrough. Over the next few years there was a succession of girls I met when I was out drinking. I would wander around until I saw a girl that looked as lost as me, and we would move toward each other, smiling, knowing what was going to happen, knowing that tonight at least we would have achieved something. We would be like everybody else. There were thousands of people for whom these things didn't come easy, people that had to push themselves and who thought too much about what they should be doing for it ever to be natural. We were lucky to live in a country where being drunk demonstrated your bona fide status as a fun person, a normal enthusiastic member of society, who would puke and cry and do stupid things like everybody else. Drink opened a door, maybe not to the world of your more enthusiastic dreams but to a place where you could get your head down for the night. Not the French film scenario, approaching mysterious girls in coffee shops and ending up in a shadowy bedroom within the hour. Not the joy of being approached—how much easier that would have been.

I thought about it sometimes though. An alternative world where the words would come to me in the right order at the right time. I would be cool and still and show her what I wanted and she would respond. Wandering around, I thought about how it would work. Me and a girl together, laughing, close, her whispering into my ear, talking about the rest of them. The other people who weren't in on it all. Not a part of our world. At night I would see us in a flat where she lived alone, a huge white-walled, hessian-floored room with a bed in the middle and nothing else. Lying wrapped around her, feeling the warmth of another person, a part of her world, listening to her breathing and waiting for my own to match it. The same depth. In and out. Together.

It seemed like it should be a simple thing, the ability to meet somebody and say something normal. To smile and be friendly and maybe even funny. I saw it in Alex from when I met him first. He was fluent, and it didn't seem to cost him a thought. By the time we left school he'd been talking to people the way you're supposed to for fifteen years. I tried. Set a low bar for myself and still tripped over it. I could barely string a sentence together.

"Just relax," he used to say to me. "Think to yourself that they're as worried as you are."

"You have no idea how worried I am," I said in reply.

"You see," he said. "You can be funny."

"With you," I said. "But what use is that?"

He understood better than anyone I knew how to use words. By charming, impressing, joking, cajoling, and wooing, he could achieve his goals. When he turned it on, he could get anything.

He did what I wouldn't. He went up to girls everywhere. He spoke to them, smiling, and the words came and the girls responded because that's what happens when good-looking guys make jokes to girls on the street. I would stand in the background, hovering, watching as they touched their hair and blushed and laughed or pretended that they weren't impressed. Sometimes they looked past him at me, made eye contact, and shook their heads, smiling.

"Did he just say what I think he did? Isn't he terrible?" they were saying. "What a load of charming old shit."

"I know," my look said back, "pure bullshit," always wondering if they would see through it, but knowing that they never would.

Later the same girls would move closer, drawn in to him—I don't think they even knew they were doing it—until eventually they were in his space, their attention on him fully now, and he would speak to them as if he had known them forever. I'd heard what he said. It was nothing much. Simple stuff. They were just words. An implication of intimacy. A question that got bigger as you thought about it. An over-the-top compliment. A thin line, but he got it right.

Once or twice I tried to have the same approach, the

same casual tone, the same feigned indifference. I couldn't
do it. At best I was cryptic. More often leery, lechy, cocky,
rude, and once it started to go wrong there was no getting it
back. I would walk away huffing and puffing, face burning.
I realized then that it wasn't just what Alex said that made
them respond, but much more. I didn't have it. I had other
gifts that maybe he would have wanted. I could get a job
anytime. I had math. Programming skills. An orderly mind.
Et cetera.

He told me about them, even when I said I didn't want to
know. Where they went and what they had done. It all seemed
so unthinking and easy and fun. They never lasted more than
a week or two, and when he finished with them they vanished
from his life.

"This last one," he had told me once. "Do you know what
she wanted me to do?"

"I don't care," I said. "I don't want to know."

"Filthy," he said. "I almost didn't do it. That one that you
said looked underage."

"Why are you telling me this?" I asked him. "You know it
upsets me."

"You want to know," he said. "You need to know what's
out there. What you're missing out on."

"Why?" I asked him. "Why do you need to tell me? What
good is it to me? Are you trying to make me unhappy?"

"I'm trying to get you off your arse," he said. "I'm trying
to get you out there. You should use what you have. You're
a good-looking boy. The last one said it to me. Thought she
might have a friend for you."

"No, she didn't," I said, trying to sound skeptical but not able to hide the hope.

"She did," he said again, smiling at me, turning on the charm like I was one of them.

"So?" I said. "What did you say?"

"Well, it's not going to happen now," he said. "She's gone now. That's not the point at all."

But when the demons visited him, he came to me. Sometimes after a big weekend when he hadn't slept in days, done too much of everything, when there was a girl somewhere waiting for him to show, he'd turn up at my place. He needed to be bolstered on a Sunday night. To spend time with somebody who would feed him and tell him that everything was all right. He only did the things he did because they were fun. No harm meant. No damage done. Everybody would move on, and by next weekend things would be better. He knew I'd tell him what he needed to be told if he asked, but he rarely did. It was enough to know that I was there. Watch TV and say nothing. Talk about anything at all. It made it better. All that performing, all the fun and happiness and the edgy promise of a Friday night when Sunday seems very far away. It cost him something. Not much and not all the time, but when it did, when he needed to turn off from everything, say nothing, clear his head, he did it with me. Stop talking, no thinking. Just sit on a couch drinking tea and watching the one hundred sexiest ads of the eighties. Do you remember, he said laughing in the short bursts that would mend him. Do you remember?

He was a mess. He kept pieces of paper with ideas, plans, phone numbers, names of people he met wherever he went.

Ideas for films, places he wanted to go, books he heard about that he felt he should read. He lost things all the time. He wouldn't use a wallet, so he was always dropping money. I knew the drill when a taxi driver would ring me to say that he'd found this phone in the back of his car and mine was the last number called. Endless bank cards went through the washing machine. He had no student card, so he used to get other people to borrow books from the library for him, then pay the fines for him when he forgot to bring them back. I tried to help him. I gave him address books and diaries, a wallet for his twenty-first. He thanked me and said how this was the thing that he had been lacking. This was the thing to put him right. Nothing ever changed.

He asked me about everything. Computers and bank accounts and law and history and politics and news. Geography. How do you get to Clare? How much is car insurance? What's wrong with my phone? What's a P45? What's a good rate of interest for a loan? Is astrology bollocks? As if I knew everything, as if I was plugged into the world in a way that he wasn't. Because outside of the social context, he didn't really work. He wasn't practical and he turned to me for help. I had some idea about most of the things he asked me, but never any depth. I could brief him like a private secretary so that in any situation he'd be able to offer an opinion, but really I was bluffing.

It was always the same. We knew how it was. What we each needed. The things that he would do and the things that I wouldn't. It was who we were. It was how we were together.

But I knew that I hadn't sat back this time. I had made the effort and had done everything that I thought was needed. I had behaved the way that he had always told me I should. I made the phone calls and had that one-sided secret intimacy of her talking in my ear, my whole body buzzing with excitement as I became convinced that something was going to happen. I had told him about it. I had talked to her friend and had shown that I was capable of having a conversation. I had looked for the signs that she might be interested, and when I thought they were there, I had stuck with it.

It was different because I wanted her, from when I saw her first. I had been prepared to ignore the risk of embarrassment and rejection and all those things that I was forever afraid of because of her. Because of the excitement, that thrill that I had felt on the first night, how everything seemed then to lead me back to her, I was ready to try.

Had she never been interested? Was that how she behaved with everyone? Had she been using me to get to him? Had all the laughing and eye contact and touching been for his benefit, goading him into action, telling him, "You better make a move here or I might do something with this guy."

It made no sense to me. I may not have been good at pushing myself to the front of a crowd, charming random strangers, chatting girls up, but I thought I could read people. All that time saying nothing, sitting in the corner in pubs and at parties just watching, meant that I had seen things that I wasn't supposed to see. The masks that slipped when people turned away. How they revealed themselves.

I'd known Alex for long enough, and he wasn't bad. Silly sometimes and reckless and overexuberant, but not cruel. He wouldn't punish me. He had never let me down, even at times when it would have been easy or beneficial for him.

The most likely thing seemed to be that he would turn up eventually and talk about how drunk he had been. He might try and reinterpret the facts in a way that would make what he did seem like a minor transgression. A mistake. Maybe it was. But he knew what I wanted and how I had seen her. He knew that it was different, and when I tried to do something about it, this was what had happened. Let there be no room for doubt. He knew.

Three days later I still hadn't heard from him. When the doorbell rang on the Wednesday evening, I knew it was him. I waited before standing and going to it, waited again with my hand above the lock before opening it, not really wanting to have this conversation. He looked worn out when I saw him.

"How are you?" he said. I didn't speak. "Can I come in?"

I walked away from the door, leaving it open, and sat on the couch in the living room. He sat opposite. He took out a cigarette and tried to light it. The lighter flashed but didn't catch. He shook it and then paused.

"Do you want one? Do you mind if I do?" he asked. I shrugged, and he put it down.

"Are you pissed off?" he said after a bit. I watched him in silence, making him work. "Listen . . . ," he said.

"Don't you start," I said. "Don't you fucking even talk to me. You and your talk. Don't you say anything."

The anger in me came out of nowhere. We sat there, him

leaning on his knees looking at the ground in front of me, his shoulders slumped and not much of an expression on his face. I wondered if I let him speak how long it would be before he started explaining himself and what I would do then. If I didn't think, I could find myself hitting him. Just swinging at him, not knowing if I would stop.

But there was another part of me that could see him leaving my place in an hour or two, maybe even three or four, laughing, everything back to normal, smiles and jokes from him as he left. The vision of it taunted me and I promised myself that I wouldn't let it happen. If nothing else, at least not that. I had to be resolved. I had to remind myself not to make it easy for him.

"So," I said when I was ready, "why did you do that?"

He looked up at me.

"I'm sorry," he said. "I can't tell you—"

"Please do. Tell me exactly."

He blew out and pushed back his hair. He picked up the cigarette again, held it unlit between his fingers.

"I'm not excusing myself, okay?" he said then. "I'm not saying it was right. I'm just trying to explain to you what happened. That's all. I'll do that, and then I'll go." He looked at me. I gave him nothing. Didn't move or speak or show anything. "It wasn't me," he said then.

I laughed.

"Really?" I said. "It looked a lot like you."

"I mean, I didn't make a move on her or anything. She grabbed me. We were just walking out behind you, and she grabbed me and kissed me and that was it. All evening when we were talking

35

to her in the pub and when you were talking to the friend, there was something there. I felt it and she felt it and I knew it was going to happen. I was going to tell you when we got outside. I swear to you, I was going to take you aside and ask you would it be all right. Because it was different. I know it wasn't fair, and if you hadn't agreed, I promise you I would have left it, but this sort of thing doesn't happen to me. She's different than everyone else."

"I know," I said. "I told you that when I saw her. Remember?"

"Yes. You did. But I didn't know that the two of us would connect like that. Me and her."

"Connect? I'm sorry, but what the fuck are you talking about? What does that mean? How many girls have you 'connected' with in the past year? Twenty, maybe?"

"One," he said. "This year. All my life. Just one. You absolutely have to believe me." I sat looking at him. He looked like a missionary about to die for the cause. Clear-eyed and overflowing with truth, so emotional that if I had reached out and touched him, I think he would have cried. He needed me to understand. He prayed that I might.

"I don't have to believe anything," I said. "I know you. It's always like this. You meet a girl and do whatever you have to do to get her and then after a week you're on to the next one. Each of them is the most amazing girl you've ever met before and then a few days later it's another story. They're all clingy and irritating and so awful you can't bring yourself to say their name, if you ever even knew it. The same girl transformed in a couple of days. You tell me all this every week."

"It's not like that."

"Yeah, it is," I said. "This time I thought you might stop and think. That you'd let me at least try before diving in."

"Oh, come on."

"What? What can you say to make me think it's any different? If you were me, how would you interpret it?"

I sat there, and he looked at me. He couldn't argue or try to charm his way out of this. He couldn't make a joke to defuse the situation. Without his usual repertoire, he was lost. The two of us sat in silence, waiting to see what would happen.

"I don't know," he said eventually. "It just wasn't like that. I didn't weigh it up and decide that what I wanted was more important."

"That's exactly what you did. It has to be. Look what happened."

"No, David. No. I had no option."

"Are you joking?"

"I didn't. You have to know that I wouldn't have done this if there had been any other way. You are my friend. You know I wouldn't hurt you. I care about your feelings. I'm not a complete fucking animal. But things just happened the way they did. That's all. I know what you wanted, and I wish it could have worked out for you, I really do, but it wasn't going to happen. I know from talking to her that it wasn't. Do you think I intended things to end up like this? Of course I didn't."

The nightmare of what he had said took a moment to sink in.

"What did you say to her? About me?"

"Nothing. I just know she didn't realize that you were interested. It wasn't on her mind. She was there because of me—"

"Jesus Christ."

"—and I know that may hurt you and I wish I could do something about it but I can't. She came along that night to see me. I realized it as soon as we started talking and then I saw that I was there because of her as well. It wasn't planned or calculated. It's just how it worked out. I'm not saying it's fair, and if the situation was reversed I know I'd be as upset as you are, but it's just bad luck that you liked the same girl. That's all. I'm so sorry, but I love her. I can't tell you anything more than that."

"Love?" I said. "For fuck's sake."

"Yes. Love. That's it."

"Okay," I said. "That's enough for me now." He looked at me, and I saw hope in his face for a moment. He thought that it was over, that in an instant I had believed and forgiven. He could be so stupid. "There's no point in talking about it anymore, is there? You've told me everything."

"Do you understand?" he asked.

"No, I don't," I said, "but you're not going to say anything to change that."

He stood up.

"I know what you wanted, David, but this is how it's turned out. I'm not messing around. This is different. I'll give you a ring next week sometime." He took a step to the door and then stopped. "And she doesn't know that you were interested in her. She didn't know and I didn't tell her."

"Why would you tell her? For Christ's sake, don't make out that you did me a favor. It's no consolation."

"I'm sorry," he said one last time, and he was gone.

I sat there and replayed the conversation. Relived it. Cut out the irrelevancies. Broke it down into good and bad. The sinner and the sinned-against. A two-dimensional cartoon world. The clarity and simplicity of a reduced moment was what I needed. Rage could turn this murky depressing dilemma into something that I could evaluate and judge. Let the mob rule of my emotions sort it out. Burn away the detail. I thought myself into a fury. It was simple. It made sense to me. We could never get back to where we had been. It was certain. I couldn't trust him, with his talk of connection and love and bad luck. He didn't value me as a friend. That was over. It was almost a relief, not to have to deal with the situation but to begin imagining a future without him around. There were other people. I had friends. There were alternatives. With my finals coming up I would have enough to think about. Cut him out. Clean. I stood up and stretched. For the first time since the Saturday, I left the flat and walked to the supermarket.

But rage burns out if you don't keep feeding it. When you come back only hours later, all that's left are ashes and no memory of the heat that you're sure you felt before. I wouldn't have the energy to sustain my anger. I knew that quietly, reluctantly even, when I was deciding that I would eliminate him. I knew somewhere in the back of my mind that in time a different version of this would begin to unfold and insinuate its way into my consciousness, one that was more nuanced and subtle and sensible. One that realized that big sweeping gestures aren't always the right way to go, that would consider the possibility that if the situation had been reversed then I might have behaved the same way that he had. I might recognize that to lose my closest, oldest friend, would damage and hurt me no matter what else I felt, and I might see that I hadn't in fact been humiliated, that the offense that he had committed only existed between the two of us. Nobody else knew about it, if he was to be believed. And already I believed him.

But there was another reason that the resolution of this situation was inevitable. To cut him out would mean not seeing her again, and that was something that I was never going to allow to happen.

CHAPTER FOUR

The room was in the depths of the college arts block, the farthest possible point from daylight or air, down a staircase that was used by the cleaners to get bleach and floor polishers and new mop heads from the caged storage area or by the porters who came, bickering and sniffing, looking for the spare flip charts and podiums and trestle tables that lay with broken chairs and desks along the corridor that led to our room. A sheet of typing paper with the words "Computer Lab 005" on it was the only marker. Walking in to the wheezing and coughing of the put-upon old computers, the buzz of the strip lighting, the smell of bedsit and underwashed males and bad coffee and hot printers, I would feel my heart slow slightly. I would breathe deeper. A feeling of comfort, if not happiness. My own space.

There were deadlines coming. The end of the term was weeks away, and projects had to be delivered. They would contribute to our final grades and follow us around in the months ahead when we began to look for work. Anything that went wrong now would come back to haunt you, visible in the facial expressions of people on interviewing panels, who would equate low marks with badness, good marks with intelligence and character and honor. It was a moral thing. The lab had been given to us at the start of the year when the department realized that leaving us to share facilities with a bunch of first-years and engineering students would result in the more motivated of us complaining and the quieter ones disappearing. They thought that putting us in our own space would allow us to bond and support each other through what would be a difficult year, and it worked. Having been independent hostile republics for most of our course, in the final year we came together as a group, united in complaint. This bunker that they had sentenced us to for the rest of our stretch, the outdated, outmoded equipment that we had to use, the contempt of the porters and cleaners and the other students, the length of the projects, the smell of each other. It was a jaded kind of railing against the system that didn't reflect how much we enjoyed being there, speaking in a language that we all understood, doing work that was vital and important and beyond every other person in the maze of corridors and classrooms that was there above us, invisible and silent, stretching into the sky.

I had been a solid performer for the previous two years, but now, with the end in sight, I started to do well. Anxiety sharpened my abilities. We started putting in twelve-hour days to make those final deadlines. I arrived with the same black rings under my eyes as everybody else, drank the same burnt sugary coffee, and ate the same cling-filmed sandwiches and sweaty pastries. I sat on the same discarded breeze blocks outside the fire exit and smoked the same cigarettes and hid my nausea. We played games on the network and sniped at each other, shot each other in the head from balconies, through trellises, suspended from wires. At some point that we all instinctively recognized, we would stop playing and get back to work for a few more hours. Complaining, yawning, stretching.

I plugged into the low-grade panic in the room, could feel the crippling stasis that afflicted some of the shakier people, cursed in their inability to settle, to concentrate, to get things done. None of them would have picked me out as a confident person. I wouldn't have seen myself that way, but I was cooler than I might have anticipated, and just smart enough when I discovered this fact not to talk about it.

Walking home in the first warm evenings of the year, I would think about what I had to get done the next day, how I could finish a project that had been nearly ready for weeks. I thought about what I would do for the summer and wondered where I would end up working. Whether I would be of a suitable standard, and whether my coworkers would be bearable. At the weekend I went down to my parents' house to wallow in their concern.

"You look so thin," my mother said after hugging me when I came in. She saw what she expected to see, the poor student down from Dublin in need of fattening. I couldn't tell if it was true. "You look so tired."

"I'm not, really. I just fell asleep on the bus. It was hot and slow."

She was putting things on the table.

"So how have you been? Not too hassled."

"Not at all."

"It's going well then?" my father asked.

"I think so. I feel happy enough."

"It'll all be over in a couple of weeks," she said then.

"Yeah. That'll be good."

"Are you sleeping well?" she asked.

"I'm sure you'll do brilliantly," he said before I'd answered. It was as if they had bought a book. Ask questions. Show concern. Remember to seem relaxed.

"Yes, I hope so," I said. "How are things here?" I asked then.

"Fine," my father said. "You know yourself. No news."

"Boring really," she said. "You hungry?"

I had no idea of what they talked about when I wasn't around, or even if they talked at all. It seemed possible that their routines were so established that there was no need for conversation, that they existed in a happy silence of familiarity. Since I'd left, they never had anything to tell me. It was almost suspicious.

In the living room later, with the smell of old flowers beginning to turn in a vase in the fireplace and the sound of the country coming in through the open window, birds and farm machinery ticking away and beneath that the faraway sound of motorway traffic turned into something shimmering and natural in the distance, I was lying on the couch reading the paper. My mother was across from me with a book, and my father was harrumphing down in the kitchen as he followed too literally the instructions on our dinner, counting the number of times he pierced the plastic film with a fork. I was happy to be there. I was allowed to have a Saturday like this. What else would I be doing?

"How's Alex?" she said then, casual, and I looked at her for a second too long, wondering did she know something.

"He's fine."

"Have you seen him recently?"

"Yeah. Well, no, not recently, but he's okay, I think."

"We haven't seen him in ages."

"I know, yeah. He's had a lot on." I looked back at the paper.

"Does he have exams as well?"

"Yeah. But he's got another year to go."

"Yes, of course. That's right." And then when I thought she'd finished, she said, "You should give him a call and have a night out." I put the paper down and stared at her. "You look like you need it, is all," she said.

"What are you talking about? Who?"

"You," she said.

"Me? I'm fine."

She smiled.

"I know that. But it would do you good. Forget about the work for a while."

"Why? Do I seem stressed? As I lie here reading the paper?"

"Yes, to me you do."

I shouldn't have asked, I should have known what she would say. I felt a prickle of agitation.

"Well, I'm not."

"I think you should give him a call."

"I'm not going to," I said then.

"Why?"

"Because I don't need to. Because I was out last week with people from my class, and because I'm busy. It's all okay. Everything is under control. But I don't need to be ringing Alex up and arranging nights out to keep you happy."

"Did something happen?" she said.

"Nothing," I said. "Nothing."

"Did you have a fight?"

"Jesus, no. Not at all. I've a lot going on, and he's busy with other things. Is that hard to understand? He's seeing somebody, so he's not around as much. It's fine." She waited again before saying anything.

"Do you not like her?"

I smiled. This was my own fault. I'd let her drag me down here.

"She's fine. That's not it at all. Just . . . nothing at all." I half laughed then. "There's no story. I'm busy, he's busy, that's it."

"Okay," she said. "But I still think you should give him a call."

"I will. When things quieten down, I will."

"Old friends, you know?"

"I do," I said, though really I didn't. Old friends what? I held the paper up and hid behind it. I could feel her looking at me. After a minute I put it down. "Yes?"

She was smiling at me.

"You'll meet someone, you know."

"Meet someone?"

"You're a good boy."

"I know I am," I said. "You are very kind. I'm not sure if I'm comfortable with this conversation, but thank you for that."

"You will," she said. "I know you will."

"That's enough now," I said.

I wasn't lying to her. I intended to get in touch with Alex. There had been messages from him on my phone that I had deleted without reading. There were phone calls that I had ignored, not to be cruel or out of anger. I just didn't know what else to do. I could think of him and what he meant to me. I could picture her and immediately the stupid hope that had been blown apart came into my head. I didn't know where I could go with it. What could I say to him? I missed him around the place but something was stopping me from getting in contact. It was a mess. If I could talk to them one time and tell them everything: the innocence of how I had envisaged it all, how much I wanted her but realized now that that wasn't going to happen. But did that mean that I had to be her friend, some nice guy that she could talk to?

I thought about her as I fell asleep, and of him, and then tried to guide myself anywhere else less contentious. Often I woke with the impression of having sorted it out, a clear sense of having stood in front of them and explained my position. I was fluent and focused. I enjoyed myself as I made well-argued points about honor and propriety and friendship in language that got progressively more complicated and unanswerable. How I had been wronged, but it didn't matter because I had other, bigger things to worry about. It always ended the same way, with me walking away as they stared after me, devastated. It was the impression of my language that stayed with me, the thrill that I felt when I was concisely summarizing the whole story in words that explained everything as it should be, with no room for interpretation. I left them speechless, realizing how grave their transgression had been. I tried to remember what I had said to them when I woke, what it was that had shook them so deeply, but nothing stuck. Then one time, not long after I'd gone to bed, I jerked awake with a bump from a racing half-sleeping state. I had just started to address him, and the words were still in my head when I came to. They were "You fucking cheating prick."

As soon as he saw her that first night, I must have realized where it would all end up. That it wouldn't be me. I just indulged my fantasy until reality eventually crashed the party and I stood looking at the two of them, pretending to be surprised that the pattern of everything that had gone before had overridden the alternative plans that I had imagined.

I kept it out of my mind as much as I could. My days were filled with study and going to college, and then when the exams started, it took no effort at all to forget about everything else. I slept and worked and did what I had to. It was exhausting. I was nervous and at night thought up questions that I couldn't answer and visualized how time might disappear, how hours would pass as I looked at the clock and watched them counting down. The reality of my days, when I went to the exam hall and was handed papers that were more or less what we had expected, had no impact on this other imagined half-life where I was always destined to fail. By the time we came to the end of them all, I was washed out, and I slept for two days, dreamless and happy.

CHAPTER FIVE

I took a few days off. I went to films and caught up with what was going on in the world. I watched television and read the papers. I spent time making meals. After a week I was ready to move on. I sent out letters to possible employers, the same one five times over. They would be hiring graduates on the basis of their marks and personality, their ability to get on with other people, I thought. How much of that comes across in a letter? I made mine sound like I was a normal person, except with an interest in banking and money and finance. It was a joke that we would all understand. It was what I would have to do, get in there and examine the numbers and formulas and percentages of percentages, and insofar as it was a project, I could motivate myself, but they had to know that nobody normal would be turned on by this stuff. And in a place like that, with dozens of people working together in a limited space, being normal would matter more than being interested in math.

Ten days later I got a letter from one of the banks. When I saw the logo on the envelope, I recognized it. They were inviting me to an interview the following week. I laughed when I saw it. It seemed so easy, and then I thought what it would mean, sitting in a room across a table from people, having to explain why I wanted to work there. I thought about it as I went back into my living room. There were the things I should say and the things I should hide and the things they would know but that I wouldn't say. There was a degree of comfort that I could see in working for a recognizable financial institution, a role that was understandable to anybody that asked what I did. I could silence that conversation. I work for a large multinational bank. Only the most inquisitive would ask another question after that. It was a job that was simultaneously recognizable and familiar and utterly anonymous and dull. It answered the question and communicated nothing. It would work for parents and family, for friends and people I met at parties. I could visualize big buildings, architecture and glass with views and hundreds of people that didn't know each other. I had no idea what kind of work they would want from me or who my coworkers would be. It seemed like a world where I might disappear.

The building was nearly as I had thought. It calmed me when I arrived underslept and shaky, wearing a suit that fit me in every possible way but still didn't look right. It didn't help that I was met in reception by a girl who struggled to hold back her laughter as we went up in the lift.

What is wrong with you? I wanted to ask her. Why do you find me so funny?

But instead I looked at the mirrored wall beside me and saw what she saw, a tired twelve-year-old boy in his father's suit with an unhappy expression on his face. When the doors opened, she led me through an open-plan office. The people that I passed didn't look at me. They weren't much older than I was, mostly men, some women. Three people did the interview, a bored-looking fellow whose smile lasted less time than the pulse of his handshake, an older guy who I thought might be difficult, and a woman who was friendly. I didn't hear their names when they said them, thinking too much about my damp hand. The woman seemed most comfortable, and she did most of the talking, asked what I knew about the company. We all talked about what I had done in college, the kind of analysis I would be up to, and they went through their questions. Then she told me that their graduate program could offer all sorts of opportunities if I was prepared to work, that they had a very fluid policy of promotion, and if I fit in, I would find myself rising very quickly. I asked about the other members of their team, and the younger guy, who hadn't really said much, suddenly lit up and started talking about the diversity of their backgrounds and educational levels and experience, and how despite that they all could progress in a company like this. People got on well, and if I was to ask anybody out on the floor did they think the company genuinely cared for them, any one of them would say yes. Without a doubt. He seemed moved by his outburst, full of belief.

It prompted something in me. I said I liked the sound of it all, said I would love to be a part of their team and that I believed I could do the work and that I liked deadlines and challenges. Not that I liked them, but that I responded well to them. I told them about those final weeks in college when we had all been feeling the pressure and how it had brought us closer together and that had helped each of us, had lifted the weaker guys and hadn't cost the stronger ones anything. I didn't say that I was one of the strongest, but the way the sentence came out, it was implied. I shut up after that. They sat in silence after I had finished. I thought for a second that they might start clapping, but then the woman said that that was fine, and somebody would be in touch by the end of the following week. I stood up and shook their hands again and bounced out the door.

When I was talking to them, when I got going, I wasn't nervous and I'd said what I wanted to say. I had seen the place, the building full of big plants and people with ID swipe cards and work to do. It didn't look frightening, and sometime in the week before they called, I realized that I wanted the job. To plug into something bigger than myself and belong to it. I could be like those other people drinking coffee, standing around in groups, looking at one guy's screen trying to figure out what the problem was. I wanted it. Get me out of the house. Think about something else. I would get paid.

They asked me to come in again the following week. When I was there talking to the older guy, who I realized now was the head of IT, it took me a while to understand that they were giving me the job. We had a five-second conversation about money where he told me how much they would pay me and I said that was fine. At the end he said that he hoped that everything would go well for me and that he would be following my progress.

From where? I wondered as I was leaving. Would the big man in a cavernous office on his own be watching me on a screen as I tried to prove that everything I had said in my interview was true?

A day of induction. Talk about the company, their history, their rules. What could not be tolerated. What they wanted for me and from me, and what we would give each other. A little symphony of symbiosis. Then a laughing guy took my photo, and a couple of minutes later I had a laminated card with the name of the bank, a bar code, and a picture of me.

The first day, when I arrived and gave my name to the girl at reception, a guy called Frank came down and got me. He was about thirty. I could tell by the way that he said my name while shaking my hand and then grinned at the girl behind the desk as we passed that he was enjoying this. Bringing in the young fellow. We went up to the floor where I had had my interview.

He introduced me to twelve people in five minutes, a flurry of names and smiles. Some more interested than others, some too busy or distracted. There were in-jokes with some of them, oblique references to people's sexuality and unsettled bets. It was all very relaxed and informal, ha, ha. People asking me what team I supported, and when I couldn't answer, they just looked at me.

"Not much of a football man," I said, laughing stupidly, trying to let them know I wasn't a prick. "But I watch it," I said then. "Sometimes."

He brought me to a desk at the end of the room, facing a wall, away from the lifts and beyond the window that ran along one side of the room. There was a computer and a phone beside it.

"This is your machine," he said. "You'll be seeing a lot of this view. If you last." We stared at the wall together for a moment while I tried to gauge why he'd said that.

"That was a joke," he said.

"Oh, right," I said. "Very good."

He showed me how to log in. The first time I did it, when the box came up and asked me to enter my ID and the screen jumped to life when I put it in, I felt a wave of excitement that almost nauseated me. Frank showed me what I'd be doing, the folder with the five applications that I would have to test, and he gave me an overview of what each one did. He said it would be explained in more detail by various other people over the next couple of days. He would be there across the room if I needed anything. That was all there was. I sat at my desk and opened the folder.

All the things that people didn't see. The thousands of hours that went into making things operate easier, better, quicker, more securely. The amount of silent invisible effort that it took to make a company like that function. This was what I began to realize through those first few days. This enormous entity made up of a hundred thousand people all over the world into which I was being absorbed, that existed in people's heads as a one-word title and a logo, floated along on a sea of hundreds of millions of processes, any of which could go wrong at any time, that if they weren't watched and checked and tested all the time could catch on a moment of inattention, any tiny human frailty, and stall, crashing suddenly and taking more and more down with them as they fell. I had thought there would be nothing inspirational or beautiful at the coal-face of the job, that it was only as you moved out through the systems and details and accounts into the real world, the lives of the customers and clients, the businesses and enterprises and governments whose decisions influenced people's lives, that you would begin to feel the sense that this was an important company to be working for. That that would be where anything vital to be found in this business must lie. But no. That first week. The training people from the different departments told me about the applications that were relevant to them and their functionality, and in the middle of it all, I began to see beauty there.

It was about attention. Thought. A struggle against the work becoming rote, the need to stay fresh and focused. The computers hummed and clacked, but how human it was. It wasn't trying to decipher a mess of code. I could see that I needed to be sharp and constant, yes, but also imaginative and creative and meticulous. It was about making something perfect and then looking again to see if you could make it better. Immunizing it against contingency. Can it be broken? What have my colleagues not considered? What tiny detail have they let slip through? And while they've been getting in with their microscopes to make sure that everything is okay in there, what are they missing from the bigger picture? What can I see when I stand back and look at it all? Between us all, we could keep it working. In the handbook that they had given me there was a statement from some guy with a head full of teeth writing to me from somewhere in Connecticut saying that the company would always strive for excellence, and I could see it now. I could feel his enthusiasm and understand it. I was a part of this world. Every aspect of this was work I could do and, better than that, it was work that suited me. I could be passionate about it.

Frank looked after me. When people were going down for lunch, he would check to see if I wanted to come along, and after I saw that he wasn't just being polite, I went with him. We sat in a group, all the people from our floor, and talked about the work and pay and the bosses and what had been on TV, and I sat in the middle of it all and laughed when I was supposed to and kept my mouth shut the rest of the time. There was a core of people who were smarter and better dressed, who went out at weekends together and made the arrangements and seemed to know everybody from all the floors as they passed around us. And then there were the others. The ones who sat and watched and didn't speak. The split was there, so obvious, in the middle of them, and I knew where I wanted to be, but I didn't know what it would take. At lunch one day Frank asked me where I'd done my degree. I could feel the rest of them looking at me as I told him.

"Is Brady still around? Still doing his thing?"

"He is. Was he there in your time?"

"In my time? Listen to this child. I'm not even out of the place ten years."

"But you knew him?" I asked, sounding more excitable

than I would have wanted. It was comforting to hear a familiar name in a place like this, to picture the professor with his
glasses and jumper and personal smell, ready to talk about
anything with anyone, always friendly and understanding and
weird.

"Complete charlatan," Frank said. "What a waste of space."

"Really?" I said.

"Oh, don't tell me you liked him? So distracted and eager
and all that mad-professor stuff. Totally contrived. He's not
worth a fuck. Counting down the days." I tried not to let my
devastation show. I didn't think there was anything I could
say. "You don't agree?" he asked.

"No, I kind of liked him," I said. He looked at me for a
second and then shrugged and smiled at me.

"So you think I'm being unfair?"

"Yes," I said. "More or less." I tried to think of something
else to make it less bald, but after a moment of silence the
others laughed.

At five o'clock people went home. For the first couple of
days when I was still settling in, I left when they did, but then
on an evening when I had work still to do I said to Frank that
I'd like to stay back and get it finished.

"No," he said. "Don't do that."

"Why not?"

"It's not that kind of place. There's no competition to see
who can work longest. It's about organizing ourselves to get it
done on time."

"I am on time. I just wanted to get a head start—"

"What's the point?" he said, smiling. "You'll just end up

having more time tomorrow. And what are you going to do with that?"

"More work?"

"You see where it goes? You just get into a cycle where you work more than the rest of us. We don't want that. When the deadlines start coming, we'll stay back, but until then we don't."

"Okay."

"Go home. Relax. Meet friends. Do whatever you want. I'm sure you've better things to be doing than hanging around here all night."

It meant that I was home before six every day. It was summer, and there was light in the sky until after eleven. It was a lot of time to fill. I would buy food on my way back, cook it, do some laundry and iron a shirt for the next day. Then I'd watch television until I could go to bed. For a while that was my routine, but I could feel the walls begin to close in.

I went for walks. Even if I wasn't talking to other people, it was still better to be around them. I cycled to the park. Every evening there were thousands of people doing things together on the pitches and the paths and across the fields into the trees. Playing sports and jogging and walking dogs. Flying kites and taking photos of deer and chasing each other. Families having barbecues and picnics. Gangs of people drinking. Picking each other up. All these enterprises constructed so that people could be together outside in the evening, as if nobody wanted to be at home.

A couple of times a week I would go to the cinema after

work and watch whatever was starting at the time. Being on your own at a film was better, I thought. I listened to the people around me eating too loud, talking into phones, laughing at the same ads they saw on television every day. The unbalanced couples where one person didn't have the same brainpower or interest or hearing as the other. Who is that? Who is he? What did he say? This thing is in fucking Chinese. The film ruined for them both. I was there for the comfort of the darkness. The primeval excitement of looking up at big bright things happening above. Noise and light.

I thought about personal ads. I could meet someone different and forget about Camille. Somebody from another life altogether who wouldn't remind me of her. I looked at Web sites and the evening paper. There were hundreds of girls in Dublin looking for the right kind of man. Hundreds. They were very specific about who they were and what they wanted. Nonsmoker, social drinker, good sense of humor. Relaxed. Easygoing. Honest. Bubbly. Vivacious. Cuddly. Up for a laugh. Likes cinema, meals, animals, theater, the Outdoors, the Arts. Seeks similar. They all sought similar, as if Dublin was full of easygoing, humorous people trying to find each other. It never felt like that to me. I saw lots of uptight anxious hassled people trying to avoid each other. Was I up for a laugh? What did that even mean? Water balloons? Clown shoes?

And who was I anyway? "Twenty-four-year-old male, shy, uncomfortable in his own skin, may or may not have hidden depths, trying desperately to avoid hanging around with best friend and his girlfriend with whom he is in love. Better if you don't look like her. Should be capable of disappearing immediately if circumstances change. Good sense of humor. You'll need it." I gave up before I'd even started.

The summer passed by. It was easier to feel optimistic when the sun shone, when the smell of the sea came into town carrying the gulls flashing white and screaming, getting the accent right as they looped above. "Where else would you be?" a taxi driver said to me one Thursday evening on my way home after work, as the pink light bathed everything and made it look the way it should. The two of us were plugged into our roles, the working stiff heading home and the old rogue trying to think of diversions. I looked at the city around me, the bridges reflected green in the river, shimmering in a way the land wished it could. The girls teetering along in groups, tanned skin and hair and handbags. The guys passing them, knowing that it wasn't cool to turn around, but looking in the end. The night air, friendly and fragrant, telling you that it would be all right. Not to worry. That you should enjoy yourself because tomorrow would be Friday and after that who cared. The whole city, cars and people, lined up and moving around each other, feeling that everything was tonight. Get it right, and the rest would fall into place. Turn away from the bouncers, from the tiny junkies who drifted sideways through the crowd trying to be seen and trying to disappear, from the first puking kid of the night, and see whatever it was that you wanted, because it was all there.

I felt the joy of the suit. It made me one of a group. An office boy. A data monkey. Nothing to distinguish me from anybody else with an ID on a chain around my neck. I saw my tie on other guys every day, people I must have had something in common with to choose the same thing. A shade away from absolute conformity. The same level of pointless resistance. The same shoes. Too many people doing the same thing to even try and be different. Disappear into the dull comfort of belonging. The same sandwich for a week at a time, then change. People like me everywhere, in shirtsleeves, all purposeful, trying to convey that you're two pay rises better off than you look. The coffee shops where the nicer-looking girls went, where we sat on rickety stools and waited for something to happen that never did. Standing sometimes with the smokers, gathered at the front of buildings, facing different directions, hiding behind gray pillars, in ones and twos but everybody always plotting, plotting. Even on their own. When I'm in charge, it'll be different. When I get out of here, I'll be happy. When I go back up, I'm going to tell him.

This new part of town that could be anywhere, with all the languages and the gyms and the coffee cups and juice bars, international shorthand for nowhere. The buildings piled high around us, trying to tell us that they were going to be there forever. The cleaning company vans in the evening, unloading the men and women who made sure that nothing ever looked different. The green bins, the wine bars, the dead unhappiness of the midweek pubs, stuck down here as if you were on a business trip somewhere grim, drinking your per diem. Because this was another country. Going back home was a trip, five hundred yards across the road into a no-man's-land populated by street drinkers and tourists gone wrong, then cross a bridge into town. Away from this affectation that still tried too hard, not believing in itself, as if in the morning it might be gone when we all arrived. Disappeared, just flat waste ground where we had thought we were. Fifteen thousand people looking at an empty space in silence, but inside we would all be thinking the same thing. I never believed in it anyway. I always knew this would happen.

CHAPTER SIX

My job was solving problems, looking at situations where things didn't work and finding ways to resolve the difficulty. Maybe other people would have been better able to see a solution to my problem with Alex and the girl. Maybe somebody else would find something obvious about that situation that was hidden to me. Maybe they would tell me that I was doing the right thing to cut them out of my life and move off in a new direction. This job was just the start of it. The perfect opportunity to make a break with an uncomfortable past.

Or maybe if I went to the girl at the next desk and asked her to come on a coffee break and told her everything, she would know that the thing to do was to rebuild my friendship with Alex. Because I couldn't be happy without him, and it was stupid to fall out over a girl. Maybe he hadn't known, she might say, maybe he hadn't properly understood the intensity of my feeling for Camille, and if that were the case, then would it be it fair to drop him? Maybe I should go to Camille and talk to her. Resolve the situation in the clearest possible way. Tell her everything, say I love you, I know this is a surprise and it might be hard to believe considering I don't know you, but it's true. And I need to know if you could ever see yourself with me. Because if I was with you, I would make you happy and be loyal to you forever. Or something like that.

Would she drop everything, forget about Alex, and say yes? I believe you. I can see it in you. Let's go. Even at my most upbeat that was hard to believe.

When my phone rang and his name came up on the screen I would look at it and not know what to do. I never answered, and now when he left messages I listened to his voice, familiar, but already a part of an earlier life that I was leaving behind. His tone was friendly, conciliatory, and what he said was always the same thing. Haven't seen you in ages. It would be good to catch up. Go for a drink or something. Anyway. And then he'd trail off, losing momentum as he spoke into the emptiness, not knowing whether I would listen to the message or whether the things he was talking about would ever happen again. It felt like we were both staring into that silence between us, not knowing what to do. I began to get nervous, wondering if the time had come to force myself into action before he gave up on me. At work I was plugging into other people's problems and coming up with good solutions in a way that my bosses were beginning to notice. At home I cooked meals and watched television and slept. I was trying to convince myself that this was my life, when in fact everything was in a state of suspension. I had stuff to deal with and was holding myself back for no reason at all.

But then on a Friday evening I was in a supermarket in town at seven o'clock. It was the end of the week, and I was going to get a film and go home, watch it on my own, and go to bed. I had nothing I needed to be doing all weekend and was happy to keep it that way. Then, as I was standing in a queue at the express counter, behind me his voice said my name. I turned and saw the two of them. She was smiling, her face lit up as if she was just delighted to see me. My stomach turned over. Everything that was in my shopping basket seemed to communicate a message about my lonely single existence. One chicken breast. An onion. Two bananas.

"How are you, stranger?" Alex said, all upbeat and normal, for her benefit, I thought. "I haven't seen you in months. Where have you been?"

"I don't know," I said. I was completely wrong-footed, trying to think, but I didn't have time to work out how I should behave. I rubbed my neck. "I was doing exams and studying and stuff. Lying low, you know." I shook my head. "Sorry, I wasn't expecting to meet anyone. I'm half asleep."

"It's good to see you," Alex said. He patted me on the shoulder, the way he always did, and I flinched at the contact, surprised. I didn't mean to, but he didn't seem to notice anyway. "Why are you wearing those clothes?" he asked me then.

"I'm working now. I got a job."

"Oh, yeah? Where's that?"

"In a bank. In the financial center."

"Cool. What kind of thing are you doing?"

"Just . . . programming stuff really."

"Wow. So. We've missed you around the place. I was saying to Camille that you were doing exams and that, but I didn't know you had started work already."

"Yeah, a while ago," I said.

"You should have given me a call."

"I know. I know. I was just settling in and just . . . You know, doing nothing really."

"How did your exams go?" she asked.

"Fine, I think. Seemed okay. I'll find out. Trying not to dwell on it." I smiled at her, small and nervous.

"No problem for him," Alex said to her, looking at me. There was a lot of eye contact going on. "You wouldn't know it, but he's a very bright boy." I tried to smile at him. I knew what he was trying to do, and it was okay.

"You've lost weight," she said. "You look run-down."

"Do I?"

"I'm not surprised," Alex said. "Locked away for months. When's the last time you were out?"

"We went out after the exams," I said.

"That's it? Are you not going out with work people?"

"They're older. And I've only been there a while."

"So what are you doing now?" she asked.

"Now? Just shopping a bit. I'm going to get a DVD and go home."

"We were going to eat something and then go for a drink after," she said. "Do you want to come along?"

"Thanks," I said. "You're very kind, but I'm tired." Before I could do anything Alex took the basket out of my hand and put it down on the ground

"That's not a good way to spend a Friday night," he said. "Come on." He grabbed me by the arm and pulled me along. I felt myself resist. I didn't want to go. I could have broken away from him. Told him to fucking leave me be and stop dragging me. Made a scene and not let him off the hook just like that. I could have stuck to my principles, walked out without looking back and gone somewhere else for my shopping.

But she was there, all warm and friendly. If she was aware that there was an issue between me and Alex, she was doing a good job of hiding it. And it was good to see him. I felt that without thinking. A comfort in his presence, a happiness that came from somewhere very deep when I heard his voice. I knew if I thought about it I could make myself angry again, but for what? A problem that I didn't know how to resolve had resolved itself. I let myself be pulled along. It happened very quickly. I went with what felt right.

"Okay," I said. "If you're sure I'm not intruding."

"Not at all," he said.

Later in the restaurant, after we had eaten, she went to the bathroom, leaving Alex and me alone for the first time. As she walked away, the atmosphere went with her. There was a moment of silence as we sat waiting to see what was going to happen next.

"So," I said.

"I'm sorry," he said.

"Don't worry about it," I said. It hung there in the air between us, not sounding the way I'd meant it.

"No, really, I am."

"I know. It's grand. Just forget it." I tried to smile at him.

"Right," he said. "But I want to tell you this—"

"You don't have to say anything."

"I do. Just quickly." He leaned forward and spoke quietly. "I didn't mean to embarrass or hurt you, but I love her and it's not something stupid or casual. I hope you can see that. I wanted to tell you so that you would know that I wasn't just messing around."

"All right," I said. "Thanks." I couldn't think of what else to say.

"And then when I saw you in the shop. I didn't know what to do. I would have preferred to talk to you before on your own because Camille knows nothing about any of this. But then I just thought, fuck it. I'm not going to ignore you if you're standing beside me in a supermarket. After twenty years we're not going to fall out over something like this, are we?"

"No," I said. "I don't want that."

"I wasn't just being a selfish prick or putting you down or anything. I'm not messing around here. This is a serious thing."

"I know," I said. "I believe you."

"Great. Thank you. So how are you?"

"I'm fine. I missed you around the place."

"I missed you too," he said. "I did make the odd phone call."

"Well. You know. Washing my hair. Crying myself to sleep. Hard to find the time." He laughed, and that was when she came back.

"Are we finished?" she asked.

"Let's go and have a drink," I said.

"That would make me happy," Alex said, and so we went.

At three in the morning we were still out in a club full of shit-faced people. We stood around a table shouting at each other. I was happy. It seemed that the rest of the summer could be like this. Out with friends and hanging around. So I didn't get her, and he did. What did I expect? Good for him. I could find someone else. There were other girls, and now, drunk and with this situation resolved, that could be enough.

I liked her company. Putting my doomed love for her to one side, she was easy to talk to and funny and bright, and she seemed to like me. Maybe he had talked me up in an attempt, conscious or not, to lessen his guilt. But there was a feeling of something shared between us, something unspoken. All that leaning in and touching and laughing seemed to imply some sort of connection.

When he was off at the bar late on, near the end of the night, she said it to me.

"Did something happen between the two of you?"

"No," I said, sounding certain before I had even thought about it. "What do you mean?"

"I haven't seen you once since Alex and I started going out. I thought maybe you weren't happy about it or something?"

"No," I said. "Not at all. I was just busy with exams and stuff. That's it."

"But has he even talked to you since then?"

"Yeah. We've talked on the phone. Of course we have."

"I just wondered," she said. "Because he mentions you a lot and yet we never see you."

"That's just bad timing. Exams. New job," I said. "It's good to see you now."

"And you," she said looking at me.

"He's a great guy, you know?" I didn't mean to say anything like that, but I was drunk at an emotional time.

"I know that," she said. "And he's so happy tonight."

"It's been fun," I said. There should have been something else. One more sentence would have settled the issue, but nothing came to me, and then I started thinking. I went backward when I shouldn't have. "And I had projects to get finished," I said. She nodded. "But we'll see some more of each other now then. I hope."

"I hope so too," she said, and then Alex came back. Some time after that we said good-bye to each other on the street, promising to meet again the following week at a party for Alex's college class.

Chapter Seven

I t didn't take long for me to see the mistake I had made with her. It was easily done. The eye contact, the conspiratorial tone, the misunderstanding of personal space that made her stand half a step too close. The way she said my name. It all seemed to suggest that there was something about me that she had seen and liked. I found it easy to talk to her, and if the conversation continued for long enough, I was afraid I would end up telling her everything. It was possible she could see it all anyway. The touching, the easy open laughing. The staring. I thought it was all for me. Something specific and personal.

But as the three of us began to spend time with each other, I understood my error. She was like that with everyone. With waiters and barmen, with taxi drivers and women in supermarkets, with the people she knew from college that we ran into on the street. And I watched as they reacted. How they stared after her as she walked away. How they looked at me or Alex or whomever else was with her, trying to figure out what it would take to be a part of her world. Hating us for being closer to her than they were, wondering how to get rid of us. A quick bullet in the neck or a knife in the back. These people caught my eye sometimes, and I always looked away, partially because I was embarrassed at how wrong I'd been but also because I wasn't sure what I was doing there.

It was jealousy first. I knew it wasn't my place to feel it, but that didn't stop me. The private part of her being was now reserved for Alex, while what I had thought was intimacy, something for me alone, turned out to be a gift given to everybody. I wondered was she using it. She lived in a different world, one that opened up in front of a beautiful flirty girl with a warmth that would make anyone do anything for her. I saw it over and over where people bent the rules, gave her something extra, unlocked the door where for anybody else they would have just shaken their heads and turned away. "For me?" her attitude always said when somebody did something nice for her, as if it was the first time. "For me?" The hand going out, touching the arm. I wanted to believe it. It would make my mistake more understandable, what I had missed out on less valuable. The first time I saw her lose her temper, it felt like a victory, as if I'd been right and her mask had slipped. But afterwards she would be the same again, and I had to accept that it was her. Ultimately it didn't matter. It didn't change anything. I was still smitten.

She could see how it was between Alex and me, and she didn't get in the way. We each fell into our roles as if we'd been practicing for them. I was the friend with a connection that went back so far that it couldn't be questioned. She was the new arrival and a significant person. I would defer to her opinion on everything—watching TV, making tea, picking films to watch. Would you like? Can I get you? Any preference? We ganged up on Alex, making him the butt of every joke because, I thought afterward, we were each punishing him for the presence of the other. It was easy to make out that he was feckless and incompetent and disorganized, laughing at his posing, at his dropped tenners and his lost phones and his late arrivals, all flustered and red-faced and baffled by how it could have happened again. He would sit there and take it with a smile on his face, happy that we were all together and getting on well.

But as much as she tried and as much as I wanted to seem normal, it didn't always work. Some days it was just too much effort, and neither of us could be bothered. A silence would fall when Alex left the room. She maybe thought that I was sulking or didn't know what to say to her. She didn't know what was going on in my head. What it was that I found difficult about the situation.

When we started hanging around, I watched her, fascinated. There was what I could see, what I already knew. But there was the rest. The way she moved and sat. The way she talked, the shape of her mouth when she spoke and the things she said. The expressions that she used too often that I listened out for, like a private joke that only I understood, something I knew about her that not even she was aware of. I had an idea of who she was that night when I saw her first, and as I got to know her, I tried to reconcile that notion with reality. She was beautiful. That never changed. Never. First thing in the morning. Pissed and staggering. After a hard night out. Dying with a cold. It didn't make a difference. But how could it? There was no explaining it. Why even try? It was a physical thing when I saw her first, a reaction, and that wasn't going to change. She was something that happened to me.

But the rest? It was only later when I looked back that I realized how much I learned about her. The way she seemed to come to attention when she met somebody new, performing now, interested in finding what was going on with them. We talked about what was happening in the world around us, silly loose pub talk, but she wouldn't let things go, challenging people she disagreed with. What are you saying? What do you mean? I don't understand? She could be dismissive. Arrogant, even. And she'd never let the point go. She would laugh in the end, when somebody broke the discussion up so that the night could continue, but if somebody really annoyed her she could turn. Her love for everybody else would intensify a little to show the transgressor what it was that they were missing.

The more we hung around, the closer I got. She was comfortable with me to start with, and as time passed, the level of contact increased. She held me when she kissed me to say hello and good-bye and pulled me by the hand when she saw something interesting. She pushed me around and hit me and hugged me, and all that easy physical affection made me happy but also drove me mad. I would go home later with her smell still on my clothes. Alex got territorial in response. I doubt he knew he was doing it, but sometimes when she got too close to me he would put an arm around her, pulling her back to him, nuzzling into the warmth of her neck, kissing her and keeping her away from me.

She was patient when Alex and I would do stupid things together. You silly boys, she would say when we'd stayed out all night and were too hungover to speak. When we sat surrounded by rubbish and dirty clothes in his place and she arrived. When we bickered about stupid silly things that neither of us cared about. The two of us together and her looking in, all mock exasperation, humor, and a motherly affection.

But all the time I could see that they were getting closer, the familiarity that had grown and still grew between them. The silence, the way at the kitchen table in the morning he reached out without looking up from the paper to touch her, knowing where she was, and the way she reached down and took his hand without interrupting the conversation that she was having with me. The way that they managed to have me around them without making it seem like I was intruding. She knew I came with his territory, and she accepted it. Because she loved him. I could see that. Every time she touched me, every time she laughed at something I'd said, every time her eyes fixed on mine as she burst with the enthusiasm of telling me something, of making me know what it was that she had to tell me. All these moments, I could have fooled myself and chosen to forget what was going on. But the fact was that we were brought together by him, and our friendship and everything that belonged to it came about as a result of him.

At eleven o'clock one day Frank asked me what I was doing for lunch. I said I had no plans, and he asked did I want to go out and get something. At half past twelve we left the building and went out across the river to a place that he said he liked. I was wondering did the fact that he'd asked me mean that he would be paying, or was it just that he wanted somebody to eat with.

We didn't talk about work. He asked about where I came from and why I'd done that degree. He said that he had done two years of commerce before he changed to computer science. He'd met his girlfriend there, and the two of them were still together, getting married in a couple of months. He asked did I go out with anybody, and I said no. He changed the subject after that. He was different outside of work. He was quieter, seemed to think before speaking. In the office I felt that he was respected rather than liked. Too harsh. Too quick to be smart, aiming for funny but ending up sarcastic or dismissive or cruel. He had never been nasty to me. I thought that might have been because I was new, but eating with him out in the world, it didn't seem likely. After we'd finished, he asked me what I wanted to do after this job. I looked at him, unsure of what he wanted.

"It's just out of interest," he said. "I'm not going to use it against you."

"At the moment I'm still settling in here. I'm not thinking of leaving or anything."

"Yeah. Sure. I know that. I'm just asking, is this job your goal in life? There are other things I'd like to do before I die. I'm sure you're the same. That's all I'm talking about. Just a conversation."

"You mean in life or in work?"

"Both. Either. Whatever." I wasn't buying it. I wasn't used to him in this setting, and he was hard to read, but I didn't believe him. I kept it safe.

"I'd like to travel. I'd like to work in different countries. I'd like to make a lot of money. I'd like to meet a girl. Is this the kind of thing you're talking about?"

"Yeah. Sure."

"I'd like to learn another language. I'd like to buy a house. Normal things."

"But do you think you need the security that the bank gives you? You could stay with them until you retire. And get well paid for it. Is that something that you find comforting or terrifying?"

I smiled at him.

"Is this a test?"

"No. I've fucking told you. It's just a conversation at lunch. Jesus, you're suspicious." I laughed at his exasperation.

"Okay, then. I think I'll do other things in my life before retirement. I hope so anyway. I would like to work for myself at some stage."

"I'm the same," he said. "There's a lot to do in the world."

"Yes," I said, and then a second later, looked at him sideways. He threw his hands up.

"I think we'll talk about something else. This is obviously making you nervous."

"You are my boss," I said.

"Not here," he said. "Only in there."

"Yes, but you'll remember this conversation in five minutes time when we're back in there."

"I think we both will." He laughed then, and I began to relax.

"Trying to know the human being, not just the worker," he said.

"I'm ninety percent worker. The other ten isn't very interesting."

"Oh, I don't know," he said. "You're paranoid," he said. "That's interesting."

IN AN UGLY BUILDING, built on a beautiful street when they thought everything was going to turn out different, they had put in a bar. Something like a nightclub, but not quite. They called it a venue, and that made me laugh. An impression of a crap cabaret, something that you might have found thirty years ago in the back of the biggest pub in a very small town; there was such a conscious irony about the whole venture that they could have put inverted commas around the name, but everybody that mattered knew what was going on. They got the joke.

This was where Alex's class had their end-of-year party. It was supposed to start at eight, but I didn't arrive until half past nine, trying to make sure that I wouldn't get there before Camille and him. It didn't work. I recognized some of the people at the bar, guys I'd met with Alex at parties or out in town, but I didn't say hello. I knew they would never remember me—always too drunk or stoned, too busy or important to have to deal with friends of friends, the general public who stumbled unwanted into their world looking grotty.

I stood at the bar and waited. It was packed, everybody

shouting at each other and laughing over the plinky-plonky music. They were a beautiful crowd. Great bone structure. Their lovely clothes and smells and tight accents. Every word beautifully enunciated. Hey, hey, hey. How are you? Talk later. Later. Definitely. Absolutely. They were the same age as me, but it didn't feel like it. They had such confidence and certainty of their own imminent glory that I knew doubt was something they would never even consider. I was sure I was going to do something stupid, spill a drink or bump into someone or choke to death in the middle of them, embarrassed and unaided. I stood rigid at the bar and fixed my line of vision on the door.

They were both flushed when they arrived at ten o'clock, pink-cheeked and glowing, which I chose to believe meant that they had been rushing.

"Sorry," he said. "The taxi was late."

"No problem. How are you?"

"Fine," she said, leaning in and kissing me on the cheek. "You all right?"

"Yeah. Absolutely. Absolutely."

"Why are you talking like that?" he asked me.

"I've been here for ages," I said. "I've been soaking it all up."

He looked at me. "Sorry," he said again. "I'll get you a drink."

"This place is great," she said when he had gone.

"Yeah. Used to be some sort of office."

"Been here long?"

"What? Me or it?"

"You. It. Either. I don't know." She laughed. "I'm all over the place. I hope we didn't keep you waiting too long."

"Not at all," I said. "I just arrived."

"You told Alex you'd been here for ages."

"Just punishing him."

"But not me," she said.

"Not you. Of course. How could I punish you?" I was trying to be charming, but it just faded away into oddness. She smiled and then didn't say anything for a moment. Alex came back with drinks.

"Have you seen anybody?"

"No," I said. "Nobody I knew."

He looked around the room.

"There's Patrick. You remember him? We met him at that thing in Deirdre's place."

Neither of us spoke.

"Me?" I said then.

"You."

I looked over and saw the guy. I remembered him. At that party he'd asked me what I did, and when I told him, he'd laughed. "Who are you?" he'd said, too loud. "How did you get in here?" He had walked away before I answered, bored even by his own question. I was left standing on my own, a crowded room looking at me, wondering. I saw him later pissing off the balcony.

"I don't think so," I said.

"I'll get him. Introduce you," Alex said to her. He went off again.

"How's work?" she asked.

"Good," I said. "Hard. Long hours, but it's interesting. It's a good crowd of people. Better than I thought it would be."

"That's great."

"What about you?" I said. "Are you going to . . . Do you think you'll . . ." I changed my mind. "What are you going to do for what's left of the summer?"

"I don't know," she said. "I was going to go to Paris, but I'm not sure now. I might just try and get a job here for a while."

"Paris would be nice."

"Yeah. Sure. But I don't know."

"This is Patrick," Alex said, arriving back. "This is Camille and David."

"Good to meet you," he said, shaking her hand. "At last. He's been keeping you away from us, I think. He said you're too good for the likes of us, and he's quite right."

"Do you think?" she said. "Why?"

He looked at Alex, thrown for a second, and laughed.

"Very nice," he said to him. "A fine thing. Lovely tits."

"Thanks," she said. "That's really flattering." She turned away and stared across the room at nothing. I smiled at Patrick.

"You need a drink," Alex said to him. "Come on. I'll be back," he said to us, and the two of them went off.

"Nice guy," I said.

"Is he a friend of Alex's?" she asked.

"I've never met him before."

"Lucky you."

"He was very impressed," I said.

"I don't care," she said. "Disgusting person." She was pissed off. I felt like I should do something.

"You know what Alex is like. He'll talk to anyone. He's probably losing him at the bar."

"Are all these people like this?"

Yes, I wanted to say to her. Yes, they are. Let's go now and never come back, run away and live in Paris, you and me.

"No," I said. "Most of them are fine, I think. I've met some of them, and they're okay. He's just—"

"A wanker?"

I laughed.

"Yeah," I said. "That's about it." She smiled then.

"You're very loyal to Alex," she said.

"Like a dog."

"No. I'm serious."

"Oh, come on," I said. "He wouldn't hang around with these people if they weren't all right."

"I suppose so," she said. "Still." If there is a patron saint of selfless friendship, I hope he saw me at that moment.

"There are a lot of very beautiful girls here," she said. I looked around for a moment and then smiled at her. I kind of shrugged. "You don't think?"

I didn't know what to say. "None as beautiful as you"? Puke. But then I didn't want to come across as a sexless freak either.

"No. There are. Absolutely."

"You should get introduced to a few. I'm sure Alex knows them all." I thought there was something in her tone, something that she didn't know about.

"I don't know," I said. "Out of my league, I think."

"Do you want me to say nice things about you?"

"No," I said. "Although . . . No."

"I will if I have to." She was looking straight at me, unsmiling, but I knew she was just trying something, seeing what I would do.

"No, please don't. It's just with work and all, I don't have time now for a girlfriend."

"I don't think that's the right attitude."

"It'll settle down in a while," I said. "Then maybe I'll try and find someone."

"You know, Fiona really liked you," she said quickly.

"Me?" I said. "She liked me?"

"She did. You sound surprised."

"I am a bit, yeah."

"Is it so unlikely?"

"I suppose not," I said. "I'm just not very good at reading these things."

"So what do you think?"

I smiled. She was pretending to be casual, but I knew that whatever I said would be analyzed.

"I think she's nice."

"Nice?"

"Yeah."

We looked at each other in silence. She laughed out loud then, a big laugh.

"You're funny, David," she said. "I can't read you at all."

"I know. And I can't tell you how happy that makes me." I saw her think for a second, then Alex came back alone.

"I'm sorry," he said. "I couldn't get rid of him."

"What a fool," Camille said.

"I know. He's not normally that bad." She looked at him, skeptical.

"He left an impression," I said.

"He's just drunk. He was trying to be nice. I'm sorry. I shouldn't have brought him over."

"You shouldn't."

"He's an artist," Alex said.

"Is he?" she said. "Well there's more to being an artist than growing your sideburns and talking like a sex offender."

"I'll tell him that," he said. "Have you been all right anyway?"

"Yeah. Fine. Talking with him," she said, pointing at me.

"And how is he?"

"Mysterious."

"This guy? Really?" And the two of them looked at me, like I was something in a cage.

THE WEEKS FELL INTO a pattern. He would ring me every couple of days, and I called them at the weekends. Sometimes we would meet before they went on somewhere else. They always invited me along, but most of the time I wouldn't go. During the week they would come over to my place. It was small, a one-bedroom flat that my parents had bought a few years earlier as an investment when they moved down to the country. It was solid and blocky and the living room was a difficult shape, with a fireplace in the middle. It always felt like you were in the wrong chair or the couch was in the wrong position, but it was mine, I didn't have to share. I kept it clean. It was so small that if I let it go at all, I would be buried in shit before long.

That was why they came. She shared with an odd girl from home who didn't like other people. Alex lived in a flat with two waiters who left rubbish everywhere, milk cartons and fried chicken boxes and ketchup bottles. Socks everywhere. I remembered being around there watching a match and seeing one of his flatmates smoke cigarettes, tipping his ash on the carpet and standing the butts, still burning, on the coffee table in front of him when he was finished. Over and over. Eight butts at the end of the match standing tight together like skittles. I was the only one who seemed to notice.

He couldn't bring her there. I knew that she stayed at night, but to spend an evening at my place was better. I'm sure he told himself that they came because it was comfortable for all of us. That we were bonding and that he was letting me know that we could all be together and it could be fine. It wasn't awkward or difficult. I made tea and we watched films and ate chocolate and afterward he'd complain about whatever we'd just seen and then they'd ask about my work and I'd ask about what they were doing and it all seemed normal and fine. I tried not to consider that the reason that she was so relaxed with me might only be because she was so relaxed with him and he could vouch for me. I wanted it to be something else.

Sitting beside Camille on the couch, Alex on her other side, all of us staring at some film that I could not follow, I thought that this wasn't so bad. He was here, and we were back to the way that we should be, and she was so close that if I shifted in the seat I could feel her warmth against me. I could look at her and hear her speak and wallow in her presence. She was in my space now, in my life. If I had known a few weeks earlier that this was where we would wind up, would I have taken it? Or would I think that I had sold myself short? Would I feel that I had abandoned my principles or that I had capitulated, exactly because this was easier?

But what principles were those? When I'd met them that night and gone with them, I did it because I believed that there was nothing to forgive. There was no great betrayal. She was just more interested in him than she was in me—I may not have liked it and would have preferred if things had turned out differently, but it wasn't unfair. If I'd walked away that evening in the supermarket, it was easy to imagine myself sitting here alone, still feeling ripped off and wronged, alone and increasingly bitter, my sense of martyrdom and perpetual victimhood intact. Any other outcome seemed unlikely. But this was how things were now. She was sitting beside me on my couch, watching my television, holding a stupid mug with my name on it, as I stared straight ahead and took a certain amount of pleasure from the pain of my secret longing. I tried not to let it show, not to groan or whimper, but sometimes as she sat beside me she would stop moving and look in my direction. For a moment I would believe that she had suddenly realized what was going on and that everything that had happened between us since we first met at the party—my calling her, the night out, my abrupt disappearance and then arrival back into their lives—suddenly made sense to her. But then she would sigh as if she had been holding her breath and lean back and the night would continue as it had before.

He'd always told me about the girls he was with, more than I'd wanted to know. I waited for him to talk about her, afraid of it at first, not knowing how I would react, but then nothing happened. The opportunity was there for him, and he didn't take it. Nights around in my house when she was out with friends, four cans in, watching some girl on the screen start to undress, everything was the same as it had always been. Except he never took the next step. He never said anything, and I found myself wondering why. Had the relationship between us changed to the degree that it wouldn't be right anymore? Was this a more serious thing for him, where it felt wrong to share the details that had always seemed funny before? It scared me that that might be the case. It seemed to say something about him that I wasn't ready for. I thought maybe he was nervous about my reaction and that maybe I should do something to let him know that it was okay. Whatever discomfort I might have felt wasn't as bad as this, not knowing what was going on, having to try and guess what his motivation was. I tried to think of a way to prompt him into telling me, make some comment or joke about her that might set him off, but everything I thought of was too crude. And then I realized that he was sparing my feelings. He wouldn't be thinking that I wanted to hear any of this stuff. He knew how badly I had wanted her. Why then would he risk upsetting me by telling me about what they got up to? It wasn't that things had changed or that he didn't trust me or that our friendship had been damaged somehow. It was that he was protecting me from something that he assumed would hurt me. He was more subtle than I gave him credit for. But I wanted to know. I wanted him to tell me everything.

She was trying to stop smoking. He didn't make it easy for her. It was something he did, not an addiction or a thoughtless repeated habit but an activity that he loved, luxuriating in it. When we were out, I would smoke with him because he made it seem fun. Sitting outside in warm summer air blowing gray smoke up into the blue darkening sky, the tobacco sweet as it dispersed. She tried to stay off but failed. She would hold out for a while on a night out and then break.

"Face it," he said to her after a few weeks of this going on. "You're back on them."

"Because of you," she said.

"What did I do? I'm not forcing you."

"You could have been more helpful," she said.

"You're the one wants to stop," he said. "It's your idea. Don't blame me if it all goes wrong."

She took cigarettes from him or from me, always saying she was going to buy some. She wasn't even thinking as she said it, five times a night. It became a joke between Alex and me. The phantom pack. In his place one night, I was about to leave. We were sitting in the living room with the light on after a video, blinking. He lifted the pack off the table and took one out.

"Can I?" she asked, leaning forward, hand out.

"Sure." He gave her one, then lit it.

"I'll get some later," she said.

We laughed.

"What?" she said.

"Ah yeah," he said. "Of course you will."

"What? What's funny?"

"You've been saying that all summer," he said.

"You don't believe me?" she said.

"Well, there's been no sign of it."

"It's a joke," I said. "We're just messing."

She jumped up and walked out of the room. We heard the front door of the flat open but not close. The two of us looked at each other.

"What was that?" he asked. "Was she pissed off? Is she gone?"

"I don't know," I said. We sat in silence waiting for something to happen. For a decision to be made. Like we were both holding our breath.

"I'm going to ring her," he said, but when he dialed her number, her phone rang in her bag, which was on the ground beside the couch. "I suppose we wait," he said, and then she was back in the doorway, standing looking at him.

"Where were you?" he asked.

"There," she said, and she threw a packet of cigarettes at him hard. It bounced off his head. "There's your cigarettes, you fucker." It was ferocious. She said nothing else, just left.

"For Christ's sake," he said, and then neither of us spoke for a moment.

"It was a great shot," I said.

He stood up and grabbed her bag.

"I better go after her."

"Okay," I said.

The next day they turned up on my doorstep. She was standing in front of him, looking up at me from under her hair.

"Hello," I said.

"Hello," she said.

"Are you all right?"

"I'm sorry." She stepped forward and hugged me. I tried not to melt into the warmth and the smell of her.

"For what?" I said. "I'm sorry for laughing at you."

"It was stupid. I just got annoyed. I don't know why."

"Because you're a head case," he said somewhere behind her. I couldn't see him because she was still wrapped around me.

"Did you think I'd gone mad?" she asked into my neck.

"No. I thought you were—" I stopped, trying to find the right word. "Magnificent," I said in the end, and I could feel her laugh.

"You don't know the half of it," Alex said as he walked by us on his way to the fridge.

CHAPTER EIGHT

O n a sunny Thursday I met him for lunch. We bought food and ate it in the park, watching girls from offices pass by in twos and threes, trying to look like they were having fun, tinkling laughs and louder conversations, being interesting because they knew they were being watched. He smiled, and they smiled back, but they all kept walking.

"I don't know why you bother," I said to him.

"What?"

"Are you not embarrassed?"

"Why would I be embarrassed? You think people shouldn't look at each other, you mad fucking fundamentalist?"

"I'm trying to eat," I said. We watched as out on the street the traffic light changed and another group approached. "What are you trying to do, anyway? What are you hoping for?"

"Nothing," he said. "It's just fun."

"If one of these girls came over and sat down here, what would you do?"

"I'd put her in a taxi and take her home."

"No, you wouldn't."

"Of course I wouldn't. I have a girlfriend, you know?"

"I know," I said. "I've met her."

He laughed to himself, mouth full of sandwich, as if he were alone watching television in the dark. When we finished eating, we moved onto the grass and he lay on his back, watching through half-open eyes.

"I might stay here all afternoon," he said.

"Yeah, well, I have to go back," I said. "Busy day."

"You should stop with that whole thing," he said. "It's making you boring."

"How's that?"

"For starters, you like wearing a suit. You walk differently when you're wearing one. You're a happy drone."

"That's not true," I said.

He sat up, leaning on one arm, looking at me.

"I think it is."

I laughed.

"People treat me better in shops," I said. "That's the only difference."

"You sellout."

"Says the young Communist who lives off cheques from his parents."

"They're loans at a favorable rate," he said.

"So are you just going to hang around here all summer?" I asked him then.

"Here? In this park?"

"In Dublin."

"I don't know. Depends."

"On what?"

"If there's any jobs going. College. Stuff like that. I wouldn't mind going away. America or something."

"To work?"

"Yeah."

"Actual work? Normal work?"

"What do you mean?"

"Like in a bar. Or painting. A job, you know?"

"Well, if something came up in film it would be great. New York, you know? Me and her. Living together on our own away from everybody, doing our own thing. It could be great."

"Yeah. It could be. I didn't know you were thinking about this."

"You know what it's like," he said. "We're always with people. Her friends and my friends and out all the time. It's never just us." I turned to look at him, lying there on the ground in front of me. I'd only just got her back into my life, and he was going to take her away again. "I don't mean you," he said, seeing the look in my face and mistaking it for umbrage. "You're cool. You don't get in the way or anything."

"I'm glad to hear that."

"But it could work really well." He was getting enthusiastic now. "Get a flat in Greenwich Village or something."

"Do you know how much that would cost?"

"How much?"

"I don't know. More than you can afford."

"So we'll work. That's what we'd be there to do. Work. Live together. You could come and stay."

I had pains in my chest at the thought of it. Actual pains.

"You want to live with her in America? Just the two of you? That's a big deal."

"Yes. Are you not listening? That's the point."

"So does she want to go?" I asked him.

"I don't know," he said. "It's just an idea."

"Oh," I said. "But by the time you'd organized it, you'd have to be coming back anyway."

"Not necessarily. We could stay for a while over there. Give it a go. It would be cool."

"What would she do?"

"Work. Loads of work over there. It would be great to get out of this kip, you know. See somewhere new. Do something different."

"But you love it here. Every time you go away, you come back talking about how you couldn't live anywhere else."

"Ah yeah, but you know . . ."

"What about college?" He just shook his head. "What does that mean?" I asked.

"I don't know if I'm going to bother finishing."

"Why?"

"It's not what I thought it would be. It's just all theory and course work. It's a pain in the arse."

"I thought you liked it."

"Yeah, but I think I may have screwed up." He sat up then, cross-legged, and looked over across the pond.

"The exams?"

"Yeah. Or they were okay. But course work was fifty percent, and I don't know how I got on."

"What happened? Did you not get the marks?"

"Sort of." He wasn't saying anything else. I waited in case he was trying to work out how to say it.

"What happened?" I said again after enough time.

"I don't know. There were five essays, and I only did two of them."

"Okay." Then. "Why was that?"

"Just couldn't get into it. And then the whole Camille thing started up. In the end I just ran out of time."

"Right." I tried to think of something positive to say. "Well, you never know," I said in the end.

"I think we both know," he said.

"If you got eighty percent on the exams, you might be all right."

"I'm sure I would be. But if I was the kind of guy who got eighty percent on exams, then we wouldn't be having this conversation."

"You could just repeat," I said to him. "There's no reason why you can't pass this year. You're brighter than most of them. You know that. I've met them." He smiled.

"It's not a bad thing anyway. Waste of time me doing another year, I'd be better off getting a job now. Or going away and getting some experience."

"Right," I said.

"No point in worrying about it," he said as he lay back down.

"Probably not," I said.

It was like him. The initial enthusiasm that faded away, never followed through to the end. From when we were young. Piano lessons. Russian classes. Football training. Business studies. Film school. All of them at one time or another were the future that he saw for himself, an exhilarating moment when he decided that this was how he would prove himself to the world. Show his talent.

That he never finished anything, never made it past scales, never went to training in the wet, never learned to say more than "I speak Russian," was something that nobody ever talked about. The pets that went back to the shop. The electric guitar that he sold when we needed drink for a party. Never mentioned again. Not by him or his family. It didn't seem to matter to anybody, because everybody knew that he would get what he wanted out of life. What he had was more important. Happiness, enthusiasm, a good soul. A family with money. Those flashes where the world suddenly seemed to match up to his glorious expectations and his path became clear, they all eventually fizzled out in a moment that nobody seemed to notice. It seemed that it was the world that had failed him and never the other way around. The pure dreamer left intact. The dirty, unreliable world sullying its reputation again.

"You shouldn't give up on it, though," I said, standing to go. "You know you could be good at this. You're interested in it. It's the right world for you to be in. It's creative, and you have to deal with people. And you like the pose."

"I don't care about that," he said.

"Oh, I think you do," I said, smiling at him.

"I'm just not interested in it as an academic subject. I wanted to make films, to actually be doing it."

"And you have been. But you have to do the other stuff to understand it. Why am I telling you this? You know it's all true."

"Loads of people don't go to film school. Loads of them. Truffaut and Pasolini and Kubrick. I could spend next year actually putting in my time and doing it. Come back to college later if I wanted and finish once I'd got the experience."

"You know you could pass every exam, do every paper, and come out on top of that class. You just need to concentrate on it."

He slumped back a little and thought for a second. Then he stretched and yawned.

"I'll think about it. I'll talk to Camille, see what's going on with her."

"Do that," I said. "I'll talk to you later. Have fun."

"And you," he said as he closed his eyes and lay back.

It was a Friday when the exam results came out. I went to work, but Frank sent me away and told me to take the rest of the day off. In the college I looked for the right board and found a few people from my class. It took a while to find my name. I didn't say anything, but one of the other guys noticed me.

"You should be happy," he said.

"I am. Are you?"

"Everybody is."

We all had done better than expected. As we stood

around, the mood lifted and then seemed to take off in an atmosphere of communal relief. It was only midday, but we went to the bar.

By the middle of the afternoon I was beginning to feel a wave of affection for my classmates. They were friends to me. We had gone through four years together and now were emerging into a world that valued us. It was a happy ending. I talked with a guy I barely knew about how we had to stay in touch and look out for each other, meaning it. At seven o'clock I knew I should be going. I hadn't eaten since breakfast, and I was on the border of forgetting everything. I had been meaning to leave for hours, but there always was a reason for one more. A different crowd had arrived, mostly girls who worked with somebody, and that livened it up again just as it was beginning to flag. The two groups had merged, and I was struggling with their names. I was sitting in the corner, and there was a girl beside me. She was a friend of a girl I didn't know who was a friend of a guy whose name I didn't recognize. She was studying at Trinity and had just left her rooms so she was staying with a friend. I remembered all this when she told me, but I forgot her name. The conversation had been going on too long for me to ask again. She was from the North, and I was enjoying her accent, the odd sexy thing she did with vowels. I kept telling her that I really liked the way she talked and every time I did, she moved a fraction closer to me until our faces were practically touching. It was a hot Friday night and the place was steamy and too loud with conversation. I turned away from her for a moment, looked around at the beered-up leery happy office crowds that had forgotten that they didn't know each other. I was a part of this world now. I seemed to fit in to it. They were people just getting going, putting in the groundwork for a night that they hoped wouldn't end. All of them full of the potential that the weekend allowed them, feeling that they might do wild impulsive stupid things.

That feeling would end on Sunday night. Not for me, though. This could be the start of something, taking this girl away from the couch in her friend's place. She could stay with me, and we could just hang around and go to the park and swim and do all the things that I had never done with a girl. I wanted to do them with her. But then when I looked again, I realized that she wasn't who I thought she was. I was fooling myself, and as drunk as I was, I knew that the following morning it would all seem different. It wasn't fair.

"Okay," I said, and I sat back. "I'm going to go."

"What?" she said.

"I'm drunk."

"So am I. So is everybody. So what?"

"I've had enough," I said.

She leaned over to me, put a hand across on my shoulder, and spoke into my ear.

"You can't go now. You haven't kissed me yet." *Cast*, she said, and I wondered. Then she pulled my face to her gently and kissed me and I understood. For a second I went with it, and then I broke away.

"What's wrong?"

She was a nice girl, as far as I could tell, and she was sitting here beside me. Why wouldn't I? What would hold me back? I knew what it was, and when I thought of it again, it just wasn't enough.

"Do you want to come home with me?" I said.

"Now? It's only eight o'clock."

"I'm going anyway," I said. "You can come if you want."

She laughed at me.

"Okay," she said. "Why not?"

We got a taxi and leaned into each other in the back seat with a loose sloppy intimacy. I was talking into her ear, and she was laughing. Nothing to worry about. I knew this was what I wanted. It was what I should be doing. Getting on with things. Taking this girl home and seeing what we would do. Enough with the pining and hoping and waiting. I wasn't going to talk about me or even think about anything. It was a release. Do something. Just let it happen.

I tried to put it together when I woke in the blue half-light at five o'clock, head sticky and feeling like something dreadful had happened. It came to me in pieces that wouldn't slot together properly. I couldn't remember her name or how we'd got back here. I remembered doing things on the couch and then coming in here. I didn't know why I'd thought it was a good idea in the first place. I didn't need anybody else. I was fine as I was, just needed a week or two of not drinking to get rid of this dirty furtive anxiety. Clean water. Not eating. Make me better. I could be better.

I was thinking about how I could deliver this message to her and when would be the right time. I rolled onto my back, and then when I looked over she was gone. It was like a dream.

I laughed and then felt a stab of rejection. I got out of bed and went to the bathroom and took two tablets. In the living room I saw glasses and a candle that had burned down to nothing, a puddle of cold wax on the table. An ashtray upside down on the couch. Bits of it came back to me. It seemed to me that we had fun. I wondered why she had left, but then when I was back in bed and the painkiller began to kick in, bringing me closer to sleep with every pulse, I knew that the point of all this was that I had to stop wondering and let it go.

On the Monday I told Frank how I'd done. He was happy and said he'd let the relevant people know.

"It works out well. You've got an assessment at the end of the week."

"Already?"

"Yeah. It's a formality, really." I hoped he was right. I thought he was, because I was happy in the job and I was capable. I arrived at work smiling. That was all there was to it.

But the night before the assessment I didn't sleep well. I tried to guide my dreams to easy material, things that would help me relax, but couldn't do it. I kept drifting the wrong way, kept being interrupted by good-looking men in suits asking me what it was that they wanted. I tried to answer, but I didn't know. How could I? They were all different. I kept talking, knowing that if I stopped they would ask me again, and thinking that maybe if I kept going I could bring myself to see what it was. I thought I got it eventually. I said something, and for a moment I could see they were impressed, and then one of them, a guy I hadn't seen before, stood up and said, Of course that's what we want but what do you want? What do you want? And I couldn't say anything. I waited and waited, and as soon as I started to say the words I knew I had failed.

I was exhausted when I woke up. I stood in the shower trying to let the water pound some life into my head. When I was washing my hair I reached out to turn up the heat and it felt like I had been kicked in the chest. My elbow came flying back and hit the glass door, which broke. It took me a moment to realize that I had been electrocuted. A big shock. I shook my arm, which felt numb to the shoulder. My chest felt like I'd been running, I noticed then. I was leaning against the wall, my hair full of suds, the floor covered in broken glass, with an electrically charged lever somewhere in front of me that might be feeling vengeful after its first failed attempt to kill me. I reached out to get a towel and threw it on the floor. I stepped out, avoiding the tiny cubes of glass. The shower was still running. I left the room and closed the door behind me. I rang my father, who said to turn the power and the water off and he'd get someone around later that day. He said it was an old system and that the flat probably needed to be rewired. He didn't seem surprised that I had nearly died in the shower, or especially relieved that I hadn't.

"I'm all right," I said at the end.

"Just a short circuit or something," he said. "I'd say you got a fright," and then he laughed.

My meeting was in two hours. I needed to rinse myself and to shave. I wouldn't have time to get out to my parents' place. I washed most of the soap out of my hair in the kitchen sink and rang Alex. It was only after I dialed that I thought that he might not be up yet.

"What time is it?" he asked when he heard it was me.

"Eight o'clock."

"Why are you ringing me so early?"

"I need to use your shower."

"Why?"

I wasn't going to start explaining.

"Mine's not working. Is it okay?"

"Yeah. It's fine. No problem."

I got my suit and went out and took a taxi over. He answered the door in a T-shirt and shorts. He laughed when he saw me.

"Nice hair."

"I know," I said, walking by him. "Can I get into your bathroom now?"

"Camille's in there. She'll be out in a sec. Do you want a coffee?"

It hadn't occurred to me that she would be there. I didn't want to be a part of a domestic scene involving the two of them, but what could I do? I wanted to turn around and walk away. I didn't even care about the stupid assessment. I just hadn't slept properly, it was nothing to worry about. I couldn't leave as soon as he mentioned her name. I had to stay. I followed him into the kitchen. There was coffee in a pot. He put a cup on the table for me and sat down and picked up a newspaper.

"So what happened?" he asked.

"Some kind of short circuit. I don't know. I got a shock and I broke the shower door and I had to get out. I was in the middle of washing my hair, and I had to get a taxi over here, and I've got an assessment in a couple of hours."

He was trying not to laugh.

"What? I could have died," I said. "Electricity and water. Why is no one taking this seriously?"

"Sorry," he said. "You're all right now, though."

"My arm's sore. I wasn't expecting it."

"Sure. So when is this meeting?"

"Ten o'clock."

"Loads of time. You'll be fine. If this one ever gets out of the shower. Camille!" he shouted from where he sat. It hurt my ears.

"Jesus," I said.

"What?" he asked, smiling.

"I'm not in a rush."

Her voice called back from the bathroom.

"What is it?"

"David needs you to get out," Alex said. "He's in a rush."

"Okay," she said.

"I'm really not," I called out. "You're such a dick," I said to him then. "Why did you say that?"

"Believe me. I had to. She won't get out for me. She'd still be there at ten o'clock."

I picked up a magazine and was flicking through it.

"How are things with you anyway?" he asked me.

"Fine," I said. "Yeah, fine. And you?"

"Okay. Not bad. Tired."

There were a hundred things he might have told me that I didn't need to hear. I let the conversation fade away, kept my head down, and got on with pretending to read. We had been there for ten minutes when Camille came out. She walked into the kitchen, her hair tied back and wet, wearing a T-shirt and a pair of panties that barely covered her arse. Her legs were longer than I would have thought, and her tits were smaller. Her skin was pale, white, and the intensity of seeing something that was rarely seen, by the sun or anybody else, added to my pleasure. It was a guilty kind of joy, mildly painful, and I blushed like an idiot, but she didn't seem to notice.

"Hi, David," she said, completely casual as she went to the sink and poured a glass of water. "You all right?"

"Fine, yeah."

"He was cursing your name," Alex said. "He said, 'If that bird doesn't get out of your bathroom, I'm going in regardless.' "

"No, he wasn't," she said, looking at me with a hint of a question. She was leaning against the fridge, a pint glass of water in her hand. The gap between the T-shirt and her underwear showed a part of her stomach that I wanted to touch.

"No, I wasn't," I said.

"What happened to you?"

"Shower problems. Electric problems. Broken doors. You know." I was looking at her face, talking to her, trying to behave as if breakfast conversations with semi-naked visions of beauty were a normal part of my life. I was not doing well. I coughed.

"Are you all right?" she asked.

"I'm fine," I said. "I better get on in and do . . . my thing."

"Yeah, you do your thing," Alex said. He wasn't making it easy for me.

The room smelled of her shampoo. The towel on the rail was damp. As I showered, I thought about how it was a sad reflection that using the same towel as her would count as a thrill for me, as close to physical intimacy as I would ever get with her. And then I thought that maybe it belonged to one of Alex's flatmates and realized that I was underslept and hassled because of the meeting, and that all this messing around with showers and taxis had thrown me. Maybe the shock had taken more out of me than I had thought, I thought as I was drying myself.

"Look at you," he said when I came out, washed and suited.

"Very nice," she said. She was sitting at the table now, still wearing the same clothes. The two of them were making me feel very dressed.

"Thanks," I said.

"You clean up well," he said.

"I better go."

"You're okay for a while yet. Where is this place?"

"In town."

"So sit down. Stay. Have a coffee or something."

"No," I said, moving to the door. "I want to get ready. Thanks though."

"You're sure?" she said.

"Yeah, I'll see you soon."

"Sorry about earlier," he said.

"What's that?"

"Shut up," Camille said. "This is what I was talking about." I said nothing, just stood in the doorway looking at him.

"She thinks I try to embarrass you," he said. "She thinks you don't like it. She says I should go easy on you."

"For Christ's sake." She was blushing now.

"I told her you don't mind," Alex went on. "And that she doesn't understand the nature of our friendship."

"I tolerate you because I have to," I said. "Camille may not be so indulgent."

"I won't," she said to me. "He thinks he's funny."

"I know," I said. "He tries so hard. Thanks for the shower. I'll talk to you later."

"Good luck," both of them called after me, like they were my parents.

I spent the morning trying to concentrate on what I should say when they called me in to the assessment. I tried to come up with one sentence that would let them know how happy and enthusiastic and grateful I was. I tried to think of anything that wasn't her. Her body. Her skin. Her legs and her arse. How her throat moved when she drank. The sleepy thickness of her voice. The relaxed confident way that she stood in front of me, showing me how comfortable she was in my company, proved that she didn't know what she was doing to me, that to see her like that was hard because it reminded me of how close to me she was but out of reach.

It was as if I was being taunted by circumstance, as if I was being shown that however much I thought I wanted her, there was room for more. My desire could still be ratcheted up. This was what happened to people who wouldn't move quickly and say what they wanted. It was how fate showed the indecisive the damage they were inflicting on themselves by not jumping when they had the opportunity.

In the meeting room the three people who had interviewed me for the job sat smiling. O'Toole told me that my work was very satisfactory and that my college results were excellent. They were delighted to offer me a contract, and then he asked did I have anything to ask them. I said that I was very happy. I stopped there, and they stayed looking at me as if I was going to keep talking. It wasn't even a question, but I couldn't think of anything else to say.

WE WERE IN MY place one evening. We had been planning on going out, but when they arrived we had a drink and then another, and then we decided to stay put. I had the windows open, the sky outside was turning orange and pink, we were playing music, and it just didn't make sense to leave. Three people with two cocktails in each of them. It seemed like nowhere could be better than where we were. I had nothing more to drink in the house, and Alex said he'd go, that he'd run down and he'd be quick, before any of us could lose this buzz that wasn't just booze.

"Wait there," he said as he stopped in the doorway, about to go. "Don't go anywhere."

"Will we leave him?" she said as soon as the door closed behind him. "Go off on our own and forget about him?"

"Let's do it," I said. She laughed and the music played, suddenly too loud in the moment of silence that followed.

"You know, he's much happier since he's started seeing you again," she said then. I wondered about the words "seeing you" and remembered what it had been like for those weeks on my own. This was better.

"Me too," I said.

"He can be really moody, you know. But recently he's a lot more relaxed."

"That's good."

"Does he give out about me all the time, then?" she said, a flicker on her face that made it seem like she could be setting me up for a joke.

"No," I said. "Not at all."

"I just thought, with the two of you being so close, that he might tell you everything. All the horror stories."

"He wouldn't do that," I said. If she had been joking, there was nowhere for her to go now. I felt bad. "And I'm sure there are none anyway."

"What?"

"Horror stories. About you."

She laughed.

"Of course not. I'm immaculate."

"Well, I could believe that."

"So has he said anything to you about going away?" she asked a moment later. I didn't know what to say.

"He mentioned something about New York. Just talk, really. Nothing definite."

"For the rest of the summer?"

"I think so. I don't really know. Why? Has he not talked to you about it?"

"Oh, he has, yeah. I just didn't know . . ." She smiled. "I just didn't know was he planning on coming back."

"I suppose he'll have to. To finish college."

"Yeah," she said vaguely. "Or I don't know. Is that what he's going to do? He can be very enigmatic."

"Him?"

"You don't find that?"

"Not really. Ask him. Ask him when he comes back. He'll tell you."

"You see, it's easier for you," she said, smiling at me. "You can do that. You're the old friend. It's not the same for me."

"I don't see why that should be," I said.

"Because the new girlfriend asking about future plans means something different. There are implications. Does he want me to go away with him? What happens if he doesn't?"

I wasn't sure if these questions were meant to be answered.

"I'm sure he would," I said as casually as I could.

"Why?"

"Because he likes you. A lot. I think."

"And I like him," she said. "But you can understand the confusion."

"Sure."

"And what if I don't want to go? What happens then? Would he stay here for me?"

I needed to move back. Away. Out into the known world. A safer place.

"I don't know," I said. "But come on. You should have this conversation with him. You obviously need to."

"I'm sorry for dragging you into it," she said.

"It's no problem," I said, "but I don't know what the story is."

"I needed to talk about it with somebody, and I wasn't sure if I should say anything to him. I don't want you to think that I'm conspiring against him. It's just that I wanted to know what you thought."

"You should ask him," I said, more definite now.

"I will," she said. "Thanks for that. I feel better after it."

"Good."

When Alex arrived back a couple of minutes later, we tried to get back to where we had been before, but we couldn't. We drank until we ran out again, and then they left.

ALEX RANG THE FOLLOWING week.

"Here's the thing," he said. "Camille wants you to come out with us next Friday."

"Okay," I said. "I think I'm around."

"She's going to see if Fiona's free." He didn't try to sound casual about it. I said nothing, trying to work out what this meant. "Hello?" he said then into the silence.

"I'm still here," I said.

"So?"

"So what? I don't know. What does she think will happen?"

"Who? Fiona?"

"Or Camille or whoever. What's this about?"

"I don't know. I think she likes you or something."

"She hated me when I met her first."

"Well, she seems to have got over it."

"Why does she have to like me?" I asked.

"Really, I have no idea. It doesn't have to be a big deal. We go out. Have a few drinks. You might have fun."

"Fun," I said. "For fuck's sake."

"What's the problem?"

"I don't want to do it."

"Okay. That's fine. You don't have to come if you don't want to."

"Ah, no," I said. "You're wrong. I'm stuck now because you've asked me. If you go back and tell Camille that I won't go, she'll think I'm being difficult, and Fiona ... I don't know what she'll think, but it won't be good. She'll think I'm rejecting her."

"You are rejecting her," he said.

"I'm not. I just don't want to do it. For whatever reason, I just don't."

"All right. Don't worry about it. Fiona doesn't even know that anything was planned."

"Really? Are you sure about that?" He paused long enough for me to speak again. "So there's room for doubt?" I said.

"I'm pretty sure Camille wouldn't have said anything."

"I'm pretty sure they're talking about it now. Right now. My ears are burning."

"Oh, stop whining," he said then. "Your friends want to

meet you in a pub, and there'll be a girl there who fancies you. What's the problem? Do you not like her?"

I barked a laugh at him.

"As if I'd tell you."

"I'm not going to say anything."

"Even if I believed you, I wouldn't fall for that."

"Why?"

"Because you'll tell Camille. If she asks, you'll tell her."

"Maybe," he said. "She can be quite persuasive." He laughed a dirty little snigger that I didn't want to be hearing.

"Enough. Good-bye."

"So it's a no."

"Yes," I said. "It's a no."

CHAPTER NINE

Into a normal happy afternoon, right at the moment that I was beginning to think of home, O'Toole arrived suddenly, standing beside me, smiling in a way that made me unhappy. I hadn't heard him come over, hadn't noticed the dip in atmosphere that should have let me know he was near.

"Mr. O'Toole," I said, trying to remember what I'd been doing as he arrived.

"Hello, David. How are things?"

"Fine. Everything's fine."

"The work is okay?"

"It's great. I think, or I hope." It was a good time to stop. If he had something to say, he would say it. He had come to me.

"Can you show me what you're working on?" He pulled a chair over and sat beside me. I talked him through it, stammering and tripping over the words, but he could see what I was doing. He asked a couple of questions, buzzed his wordless approval, but mostly he just watched for five minutes. I was letting one of the processes run, waiting for it to do its thing, when he spoke in a quick quiet voice.

"I'm having a few people over on Sunday afternoon. Barbecue or something. Depending on weather. It would be good if you could be around."

"Em . . . ," I said, thinking. What was this?

"Or are you busy?"

"No, I'm not. That would be great. Thanks very much."

"Right. I'd prefer if you didn't say anything to anyone else."

"Okay. Sure." He handed me a card with an address on it.

"About three?"

"Okay," I said.

"See you then." He got up and left without looking back.

"What did he want?" one of the girls asked as she passed.

"I don't know," I said, my face reddening. "Just checking what I was doing."

"He wants to fuck you," Alex said later in a bar when I told him about it.

"No, he doesn't," I said. "He's married."

"So what? He can't fuck you because he's married?"

"That's not it. That's not what it is."

"So what do you think?" he asked.

"I don't know. I thought maybe he wanted me to work at it."

"Doing what?"

"Like a barman or waiter or serving food or something."

"He would have asked you if that's what it was," Alex said.

"He's your boss. You work for a bank. He's not going to hire you for a cash-in-hand job at his house doling out canapés to his friends. Really."

"I don't know. I thought then that maybe it might be a way of firing me, you know? He said there'd be a few people there. Why would he not want me to tell anyone about it?"

"I thought you had your assessment. They told you they were happy."

"Yeah, but I haven't signed anything. They should have given me a contract by now, and they haven't. Maybe he's changed his mind."

"Why would he? And even if he had, why would he invite you out to his house to fire you?"

"I don't know. To soften the blow?"

"It doesn't seem likely," he said. "Why wouldn't he just do it at work?"

I hesitated. "Because he's a nice guy?" Even saying it I could see that it sounded stupid.

"No. That's not it," he said.

"I can't think of anything else."

"I don't know why you're so paranoid. You've been working hard for them, doing a good job. Why wouldn't he want to get the best guys over and do something nice for them as a show of appreciation?"

I could imagine that he was right. I wanted to believe him.

"What do you think I should wear?" I said then. "He's my boss, but he said it was a barbecue. Am I supposed to wear a suit to a barbecue?"

"Definitely not."

"You think?"

"It'll be casual. You should wear a thong and nothing else," Alex said. "Wait and see. I bet I'm right."

He'd rung me at home to see if I'd come out for a couple. I didn't want to, but he pushed. After half an hour of talking about nothing, I was wondering if I should ask him if he was all right.

"This going-away thing," he said at last. "It's wrecking my head."

"What's the problem?"

"She's on at me now. First it was the parents, and now she's started. Fucking college."

"What about it?"

"She's saying that she thinks I should go back and repeat the year. I wanted to go away with her. I said it to her before, and she was cool with it, but now she's changed her mind."

"Why?"

"I don't know. She'd started out saying that she wasn't sure if she wanted to spend a year away, and then when she heard what my parents were saying, she jumped on it, and now she's saying that the only thing I should be doing is this."

"You don't agree?"

"Of course I don't agree. It's a waste of time. I'm talking about going and doing the work—getting a job in film, starting to actually do it—and she's telling me that the course is a better way. It's safer to have the qualification. Safer. For what? But I can't do another year of it. I can't." I smiled at him. "What?"

"You shouldn't say you can't, because actually you can."

"Okay. I don't want to. I've had enough. For some reason, the first time that I've had a clear idea of what it is I want to do, when I know the right path to take, everybody's pushing against me."

"Not everybody, surely."

"Camille and my parents. They say I have to finish it. They say that now. When I started, they were happy enough for me to check it out, see how it suited me."

"Were they? I don't remember that."

"I thought they were." He said nothing for a moment. "I suppose you're going to tell me the same thing."

"No," I said. "It's up to you."

"I've got to get out of here. I've been wasting my time in this place for too long. I need to do something."

"Then do it."

"I wanted her to come," he said, but he wasn't really talking to me now. "It would have been cool, but she's not going to. I don't know if she's trying to force me to stay or something."

"Force you? Maybe she just doesn't want to commit everything to going away for a year. It's a big deal."

"I know that," he said. "But still I want to do it with her. Just, she doesn't feel the same way."

"You haven't been going out that long, and what you're talking about is living together. Three thousand miles from home. If you did the year again, the two of you could go next summer. New York will still be there."

"I'm not doing it, David. That's fucking it."

"Okay. Relax." He held his head, his elbows propped on the counter.

"They won't give me the money," he said then. "They'll pay for me to go to college, but not to go away."

I laughed.

"What?"

"That's kind of fair enough."

"What am I supposed to do?"

"I don't know. Get a loan. That's what banks are for."

"Banks won't give me money to fucking disappear in America."

"Okay. So you've got a problem."

"I know. That's why I'm here." We sat in silence for a minute. "Did you say something to her about me?" he asked then.

"No. What kind of thing?"

"That I never finished anything."

"No. Of course not."

"Because she said that to me. We were talking about it and she said that, and I don't know where she got it."

"Not from me."

"You know this was different, don't you? You know I tried. I've been good. I haven't been fucking around."

"I know," I said.

"I really tried. This is a nice idea, and she doesn't even have any plans for the year yet. But she's telling me I should finish college, like she's my mother."

"Maybe she thinks this is the best for you both in the long run."

"But is she going to be here in the long run? I swear to you, I've really tried with her. It was going so well, but this is going to be the end of it. I'll go."

"Why? Why now is it so important? You've always been happy here. Haven't you? You have a good time. What's changed?"

"I've spent too long getting my shit together. You're working now. All my own crowd are away. I need to make a break. Get away."

I'd heard this before. The same worries. The same resolution to change. Life to begin again somewhere else, fresh and clean and new. People didn't know this about him. They thought he just drifted along, happy with how things were.

"You could come," he said then. "If she doesn't, you could."

"Should I be on standby in case she says no?"

He smiled a little apology.

"I don't mean it like that. But if I'm going to go anyway and she doesn't want to, we could go together. You could get any job you want over there, you'd be right in the thick of things."

"This job," I said. "It's a big deal. I can't just leave."

"Think about it," he said. "It could be a lot of fun."

"She may change her mind. Talk to her."

"I talk to her all the time," he said. "We talk enough."

"I don't want to get in the middle of it," I said. "You know I hope it works out the way you want, but she's a friend now as well, so—"

"So what? She can look after herself," he said. "You don't need to be worrying about her."

"I'm not worried. I'm just not going to get involved."

"You're not doing her any favors."

I looked at him.

"What does that mean?"

"I mean that I see a whole lot more of her than you do, and it's not the way you think it is. It's not poor Camille having to put up with me and my messing. She's on top of it. She can fight her own corner."

"I'm sure she can. I'm just saying I shouldn't interfere."

"I'm asking your opinion." He shrugged. "You have her on some pedestal where she can do no wrong. But don't worry about her. Tell me what you think I should do."

"I think you should make your own decisions," I said, standing up.

I HAD TO TAKE two buses to get to where O'Toole lived. I found the road, but the house only had a name, no number, and I kept walking for nearly an hour as the road went up the side of a hill and then seemed to double around on itself. All the houses had high gates that I couldn't see over, and there was nobody on the street walking. Nobody to ask where this place was or if I was still on the right road. At four o'clock, as I was starting to panic, I saw it, the name in wrought-iron letters on a white wall and wooden gates that were closed. There was a buzzer on the wall and I pressed it. It made no noise. I listened and could hear nothing, then a crackle and a voice said hello.

"It's David Dillon."

"Who?" the voice asked.

"David Dillon?" I said again as if my name was a question. "Mr. O'Toole invited me?"

"Hold on."

After ten seconds of silence the gates began to open. I waited to see who was there, but there was no one, so I started walking up the drive. It was an avenue with trees on both sides, the sun twinkling through, and then I saw the house, low and modern and not what I'd expected. I still couldn't see anyone, but I could hear voices and followed them around to the back. A group of ten people sitting around in garden chairs under umbrellas, drinking beer and wine. I saw Frank and a couple of others that I recognized. O'Toole was sitting at a table with a woman who could have been his wife and an older guy, seventies maybe, who was smoking a cigar. The three of them were laughing in the sun, glasses in their hands. On a patio behind them there were two Asian guys cooking at a grill. O'Toole stood up and waved when he saw me. I walked over, and he came to meet me.

"David. You're good to come."

"Not at all. Thank you."

"Did you have trouble finding the place?"

"Ah, no." Then I thought of the time. "Just, it's a long road."

"If you don't know where you're going. You should have called."

"It wasn't a problem," I said. "I hope I'm not too late."

"You're fine. Come over here." He led me by the elbow to the woman and the old fellow.

"Marie. This is David Dillon. He started with us in June."

She looked up at me, shading her eyes with her hand.

"Hello."

"And this is Mr. Donnelly."

"Hello," I said, shaking his hand. It was sweatier than mine.

"David is a programmer. Just out of college. He was top of his graduating class."

"There were a few of us—," I said, and then stopped.

"Modest," Donnelly said. "Very good. Our kind of man." He chortled to himself and O'Toole smiled.

"Do you want to get a drink?" O'Toole said to me. "The boys will look after you. Frank is over there. Go and relax. There'll be food in a little while. I'll talk to you later."

I walked away, leaving them sitting in a moment of quiet as they let me go. I got a beer from one of the Chinese guys and went over to Frank.

"Hey, young fellow," he said. "Good to see you."

"And you." He didn't seem at all surprised that I was there, as if we met on this lawn every week. "Have you been here long?" I asked him.

He shrugged and smiled.

"Are you having a pleasant afternoon?" he said. I thought he might be drunk.

"Sure," I said. "I think so." A chair arrived behind me before I knew what was going on. I sat in it between him and a girl.

"Hi, David," she said. I'd seen her around the office but had never spoken to her. She was rubbing sun cream onto her legs. Frank had gone back to talking to the guy on the other side of him, his interest in my arrival having passed.

"I'm sorry," I said to her. "I don't think I know your name."

"It's Sara."

"Good to meet you."

"Yeah. Hi."

"So," I said, and then there was nothing. I had no idea what was going on. Were they members of a cult, or Masons, or were we all going to take our clothes off after lunch and see what happened? Sara was rubbing cream into her arms now, pushing up the sleeve of her shirt to get at her shoulders. She moved her seat back out of the shade and sat facing the sun with her head back and her eyes shut. I didn't know if I was allowed to talk to her. On the other side Frank and a couple of other people laughed. Big happy laughs. Fuck them, I thought.

"What do you do?" I asked her.

"Me?" she said, without opening her eyes.

"Yes."

"Product development," she said. "Same kind of thing that you'll be working on."

"Oh, right. And how is it?"

"It's great." She sat forward again and opened her eyes, looked at me. "It's a good job. I love it, but I don't know how long I'll be there."

"Really?"

"I don't know," she said. "It depends on how things work out."

"Okay." I had no idea what she was talking about. I wasn't sure if I was supposed to ask, if that was what she would expect, or if she was just weird. She didn't seem to need anything else from me.

"And you," she said after a minute. "Where did you come from?"

"How do you mean?"

"Today."

"Oh. From town."

"Taxi?"

"Bus."

"Great." She laughed.

"Two buses, actually."

"Even better. That must have been fun."

"It took two and a half hours," I said, and she laughed again. Bizarrely, this conversation was beginning to go all right. We talked for fifteen minutes, and she became more normal. She had gone to Trinity, had worked in Kenya for a year, and came back because she thought if she'd stayed there any longer, she might have stayed forever.

"And what's the problem with that?" I asked her.

"Kenya," she said. "Have you been?"

"No."

"Then you don't understand."

"That's why I'm asking," I said, trying to keep my voice happy.

"I don't know," she said. "Wasn't the way I wanted my life to go."

When we went up to get food, Frank asked me how things were going. I said it was fine, everything was great. We sat down together, and he was talking about how Sara was deeply brilliant, the most talented person he'd ever worked with.

"What did you think of her?" he asked me.

"Nice," I said.

"Isn't she? Bit of a nutcase, though."

I hesitated.

"It's okay," he said. "She is."

"Maybe a bit."

He smiled at me. It nearly made me cry.

"What is today about?" I asked him before I could stop myself.

"What?"

I leaned in to him and said it quietly.

"Why am I here? I don't understand it. I don't know who any of these people are. O'Toole told me not to tell anyone that I was coming. Did you know I was going to be here?"

"Yes."

"So what's it for?"

"It's nothing to worry about," he said. "Just relax. It's all fine."

"Why do people keep telling me to relax? I'm going to have a fucking panic attack in about ten seconds."

He looked at me then. He must have seen that I was lost and I didn't know what was happening.

"Everything is fine. O'Toole will talk to you later and tell you what it's about, but it's all good. I shouldn't say anything more than that. I'll let him sort you out. You don't need to worry. This could be a very happy day for you."

"If what? What do I have to do?"

"Nothing. Just have a drink. Tell me what you did last night. Talk about your family. Anything."

"Okay," I said. What else could I do? He asked again about what I'd got up to the previous night, and when I said I'd stayed in, that I hadn't done anything, he told me about where he'd been. When O'Toole came over, I was feeling almost normal.

"Can I have five minutes, David?" he said.

"Sure."

We walked across the lawn to a white painted metal table and chairs away from the rest of them, the noise of the conversation fading behind us. He sat down across from me and started to talk. From where I was sitting, I could see the others drinking and some of them still eating.

"I'm sorry not to have spoken to you before now," he said. "You must be wondering what is going on." He looked at me, waiting for something.

"Yes," I said. "A bit."

"I'm sure. Okay. Well, the thing is this. I'm leaving the company. I'm finishing up in two months. I'll be working with my replacement getting him up to speed, and that will be it. We felt that it would be less disruptive not to announce it in the company until a bit closer to the time. I've been with the company for eighteen years, started out on the floor in London as a clerk and came back here when they opened this office.

"But what I want now is a change. I've got another eighteen years of work left in me, and I think if I'm ever going to do my own thing, I should start now. Mr. Donnelly over there is a friend of my wife's family. I've been talking about setting up on my own for the past couple of years, and he always said I should talk to him before I did. And then a former colleague from London, who's been working in IT for a lot longer than me, moved to Dublin last year, and that was the real impetus behind this. We've been putting together a plan for a software development company. We have the idea, we have the product, and the market is there. Mr. Donnelly is happy. We're happy, and we're ready.

"But we need good people. It's going to be a small operation, only seven or eight people. Frank, who you know, is going to come with me. There are a couple of others that you may not have met yet. None of this is being talked about in public yet, and for various reasons there'll have to be a certain amount of political subtlety when we actually start.

"I asked you here to see if you'd be interested in coming with us. I've been impressed by the way you've settled in so quickly, and the work you've done has been excellent. Frank speaks very highly of you, thinks you're a person of the caliber that we need. So, I have to ask . . ." He laughed, almost nervous. "Do you think you might be interested?"

"Yes," I said. "I think I might be."

"This is just a first conversation. There are things that we'll need to talk about. The good news is that we would pay you well, and there will be shares and dividends that could be worth a lot. The other thing is that it should be enjoyable. It would be hard work getting it set up, and I know it will involve long hours and a lot of uncertainty, but if it works you'll be in at the start of something that I think could become very big. In the best-case scenario, we set it up, work hard at it for a few years, grow it to what it should be, and then go public. That's if it works.

"If it doesn't work, you'll have given up the security of a job with the bank and the potential of a long and happy career with them. A young guy like you, capable and serious about the work, could move up the ranks there very quickly. I'm proof that they have great mobility for their staff, and that's not something to be taken for granted. You could invest a couple of years at this stage in your life in something that doesn't work. It could be frustrating and boring and unhappy. We could all be out of work within a year. I don't think it's likely, but it could certainly happen. Anyway. You can see what I'm telling you. With the talents that you have, I think you're going to do very well for yourself no matter what you do. Ultimately it comes down to what you want."

"I want to do it," I said, clear and straight and loud.

"You can think about it. You don't have to decide right now."

"I know that. But I don't think there's much doubt. I mean, everything that you've said makes me want to do it. It just seems like an opportunity, and I'm really grateful that you asked me."

"We asked you because you're good enough. That's the basis of the offer. You seem like a nice fellow and everything, but it's not an act of kindness."

"I understand that. But you can count me in."

He smiled at me.

"Why don't we talk about it again next week, after you've had a bit of time to cool off? You should think it over, consider those things I've told you. What you would be giving up is real. I'm very hopeful for this company but that doesn't guarantee anything."

"I know," I said. "I would be taking a chance."

"And some people wouldn't do that when they already have a more secure option."

"I understand," I said.

"I'll be in touch with you anyway," he said, standing. "Thanks for giving up your Sunday to be here. I'm sure you've other places you'd rather be."

"Happy to have come," I said. "Thank you." We shook hands. I wanted to tell him that at this point in my life it felt like the perfect thing to do, something unexpected and brave, but if I started down that road, there was a chance that I might end up crying or hugging him. I felt shaky.

"By the way," he said as we were walking back over to the party, "you understand that this is a sensitive issue. The bank would not be happy if they thought I was poaching their best people." I nodded, my face serious, intense.

"I know," I said. "I won't say anything."

"To anyone," he said as he drifted off toward his wife.

Frank was still in the same place, talking to Sara. They looked up when I came back.

"Everything all right?" Frank asked me.

"Yeah. Fine."

"Get yourself a drink," he said. "He'll be kicking us out soon."

It didn't seem to me that I had been doing more than anybody else. Nobody seemed to be slacking, and they all were capable. I couldn't think what I had done to make him notice me. I was new, and I was pretty quick. I kept my head down and said nothing. Smiled at everyone I saw. Was that enough? Would that be enough to get me ahead in life?

I told no one. I said nothing to my parents or to Alex or Camille when they rang to find out how I had got on. It was a barbecue, I said. That's all it was. I didn't see Frank much that week at work. One morning I arrived at the same time as him, and we took the lift up alone together in silence. I don't know if it was the chance that somebody else might get in, or if talking about the job in that building just felt too risky. Whatever it was, neither of us spoke. When the door dinged and opened, we walked out together.

"It'll be a quiet office," he said in a low voice, and I smiled.

I WAS OUT WITH Alex on the Friday night in a pub in town. I had stopped off to meet him on my way home; he was going on to a party somewhere else. I didn't want to say anything to him about the job until it was finalized. I was going home to watch television and looking forward to bed at ten o'clock. Nothing would keep me from sleep.

"What are you doing this weekend?" he asked.

"Nothing. There were people from work going out tonight, but I wasn't up to it."

"What's wrong with you?"

"I'm tired."

"Tired? What the fuck is that?"

"I get up at six o'clock. Five days a week. What do you do in the morning?"

"I can tell you what I do in the morning," he said. "But I don't think you'll want to hear it."

"Probably not."

"How about tomorrow? Do you want to do something?"

"Maybe," I said. "In the evening."

"That suits me anyway. Tonight might be big. There are things planned."

"What kind of things?"

"Fun things that involve being up all night and feeling very shit tomorrow."

"Fair enough," I said. He probably wanted me to ask more, but I was distracted.

"Hopefully I'll give you a call. I haven't seen much of Camille this week, so there's a danger she'll want to catch up. Quality time." I looked at him, noticing his tone. He shrugged.

"What?"

"That sounds all right to me," I said.

He laughed, dry.

"Whose side are you on?"

"I didn't know I had to pick sides. I didn't know there was a choice."

"Of course there is. There always is."

"Right," I said. "If you're suggesting that I think more of her than I do of you, then I'm surprised there's any doubt. You're rude and lazy and you treat me very badly—"

"Not true," he said.

"And she's just beautiful and fun and intelligent. There's no contest." He laughed into his glass, a bitter little private joke. "What?" I said. "Is there something else?"

"Nothing."

"You're sure?" I knew he'd say it. If it was the first drink, he wouldn't, but now he was off. Nothing would stop him.

"Just . . ." He hesitated. "You should try going out with her for a while."

"I gave it a shot," I said. "You know that." He looked at me for a second. Then nodded and smiled. As the smile faded, he spoke again.

"Yeah, well. It's not as good as it looks." I got distracted, thinking that it must be. I couldn't imagine how it would be otherwise. For all the things he complained about, it seemed to me that she just wanted what was good for him. I didn't know what to say to him now, so I said nothing. "I'm not complaining," he said then, "but it isn't all just fun and games. She can be hard work sometimes."

"Isn't everybody?" I said.

There was something wrong with him, a sadness or an uncertainty. The conversation was too muddled for me to be sure what was happening. I felt I should ask him if he was all right. Just one more question to be sure. But then he seemed to come to suddenly, the window into his vulnerability and frustration closed tight, and his face told me that he was building up to something.

"It could have been you," he said. "Complaining to me in a pub about this girl. You boring the arse off me for a change."

"I wouldn't," I said. "I never would."

"You don't know what you're talking about," he said. "You have just no idea."

He leaned forward to order another round, and when he came back to me, the evening went on as if nothing had happened, as if none of it had been said. I could feel the anger burning in my throat and in my chest. It showed in my hand that shook as I drank. I'm sure he could tell what was going on with me, but to hear him talk, to see him laughing and joking, you would never have known.

THE SECOND TIME, I took a taxi to O'Toole's house. I told him I would do it. We talked about money and how the structure would work with shares and bonuses, and he made it sound like I would be doing very well. He was less cautious than he'd been the previous week, and I was glad of it. The endless qualification of everything took the fun out of it. We were setting up a company. He told me about the product and how he was hoping that we could get a patent for it. If we did, he said, we could be talking about a lot of money. He said nothing would be happening for a couple of months, and that they were hoping to start in November, so I should aim to be available then. I should work until October and give a couple of weeks' notice.

I walked back along that endless road with nobody around me, nobody knowing where I was or what I was doing. I had fed off his enthusiasm. I believed in him and in the product and in the other people that he had chosen to set this up. I believed in myself, in my own ability to hold my own no matter what was put in front of me. Wherever it had come from, I realized now that when it came to work I was good at what I did, better than most people. If a manager with a multinational bank could see it in me, why hadn't I? I saw it now. I could see it and feel it and believe as I walked over the hill along this beautiful road under the trees past the houses with names and views and driveways and gates.

What would Camille think when she heard? For me to get a job like this, to be chosen from a crowd, to be poached in a way that had to be kept quiet, would surely say something to her. I could admit to myself that I wanted her to notice this and see it for what it was. To see me not just as Alex's friend but as somebody different, a person of value and intelligence, a prodigy. The recklessness of what I was doing would appeal to her, I thought. I was turning my back on certainty, the plodding predictability of going straight from college to a job in the bank. I was taking a chance, going with my instinct rather than my head. I hoped she would see what a big deal it was for me and would understand what it said about how much I had changed, even in the short time that we'd known each other. I hoped she would see it, because I had done it with her present in my mind.

IT WAS LATER ON that night. We were in some place in town with friends of hers, people I didn't know. I waited until Alex asked what I'd done that day, though it nearly killed me.

"I went back out to my boss's house."

"Is that a regular thing now?" Camille said.

"He asked me back. Just me."

"If this story ends the way I hope it's going to," Alex said, "I will say I told you so."

"He was offering me a job."

"What kind of job?"

"He's leaving the company and setting up on his own. He's taking a couple of people from the bank with him. He wants me to go as well."

"Wow," she said.

"What kind of thing is he doing?" Alex asked.

"It's a software company. He has money behind him, he says, and he's talking about stock options and dividends and a whole load of stuff that I don't understand. But I don't need to. Basically if it takes off, I could do really well. And if it doesn't, what have I lost? A job in a bank. I can get another of those if I want."

"That's brilliant," Alex said. "It's just great. Why does this guy want to hire you? Is he sure? Are you very good at what you do?"

"He seems to think so. Because I am. I can be modest tomorrow. He told me that I am extremely talented, and he should know."

"Good man," Alex said. "I'm so happy." He put an arm around my neck and pulled me to him. "You're a star," he said. I wanted to cry, I felt so close to him then. I couldn't say anything.

"Well done," she said, all smiley and warm. "That's great." She hugged me and kissed the side of my face.

"Thanks," I said in her ear.

"I'm so happy for you."

"So when do you start?" Alex asked.

"Not for a few months. I don't know. I can't say anything

at work. I'll just keep working away and then give notice in a while, say it's not for me or whatever. Then we'll get going."

"It's just a great thing to do," he said. "Such a cool thing to be involved in."

"I know," I said. "I hope it works out."

"It will," he said. "I know it will."

CHAPTER TEN

When I woke the following Saturday, I knew from the light on my bedroom wall that it was a day for being outside. I had a shower and went out to get the paper and a coffee. It was only nine o'clock and it was already hot, the street full of older guys that couldn't sleep any more, all nervous white flesh and shorts and sandals, out buying little treats for their families. Pastries and bagels and chocolate and strawberries. Bringing home breakfasts for the patios and balconies. I had nowhere for that, nowhere to lie around outside, but I could go to the park. I could keep walking into town and buy food and beer and go home, get a rug and something to read, and cycle over, spend the afternoon in the middle of nowhere with no one. There was a pleasure to be had in that, being out there on my own, feeling the sun, smelling the grass. The thought made me happy. I was capable of finding the perfect solution to a day like this on my own.

It didn't seem true though when Alex rang to ask what I was doing and I told him nothing, that I was around. He was working on an ad for a friend and would be finished by two. I said we could get food and go to the park, as if I had just thought of it. He said it was a great idea and that they would be on for it. Him and her. He'd ring her to check but he thought she'd be keen. If it was okay with me, he said then, hesitating, sensitive just in case, and I said yes, absolutely. Of course.

I didn't mind. It was better, I thought. It seemed like the kind of thing I should be doing. He went off and called her and then rang back to say they'd meet at my place at half past two.

I was waiting on the steps of my building when she pulled up outside in her car. I stood up when she arrived, but she sounded the horn anyway.

"What are you beeping for?" I asked when I opened the door.

"Saying hello," she said. "What's in the bag?"

"Nice things."

"How long are we going for?"

"What? Is it too much?" She laughed at me.

"It looks like an awful lot."

I stood there in the open door not knowing what to do, whether to bring some of it back up, but in the end I just threw it all onto the back seat.

"I like to be prepared," I said. "I don't understand what's so attractive about spontaneity, not having enough or not being able to open things or sitting on damp. What's so great about that? We are ready."

"What for?"

"For everything," I said. "Where's Alex?"

"Alex is going to meet us there," she said. "He got delayed."
I noticed how she put a distance between herself and his words.

"Okay," I said. "What's he going to do, ring us when he
gets up there?"

"Yeah." She didn't seem happy.

"That's all right, isn't it?" I asked.

"Oh, I know. It's fine."

"So?"

"So what?"

"Is there a problem?"

"It's not the first time he's done this."

"Yeah, but you know what he's like."

"I do," she said. "I know."

We drove across town, past people everywhere, sitting outside in front of pubs and cafés, everybody talking louder than
usual, their body language exaggerated. As we drove in her
car with the windows open, going to a park to lie around all
afternoon, drinking and eating, I could plug into that mood.

I told her where to park and then led her down into a little
valley and then up the side of a wood and across a field to a
group of trees in bloom, explosions of white blossom above
long grass. There was no one else there. I put a rug down and
took out two beers, holding one out to her.

"Will you?"

"I can have one. Right?"

"One's not a problem."

She took it and lay down on her stomach, her legs crossed

over each other bent up behind her. She was wearing a skirt that was short enough. I took out the food and started getting it together.

"You went to a lot of trouble," she said.

"It's nothing really," I said. I tried to think of some joke to make at my own expense but couldn't. I gave her a napkin and a plate. I was sitting facing the same direction as she was, looking at the trees.

"Hawthorn," I said, pointing.

"Very nice."

"You don't normally notice them. They're just boring, in hedgerows and that, but when they flower it changes the way the whole country looks. Color everywhere. You can see it from planes. The whole countryside white."

"Wow," she said. "You know a lot about hawthorn."

"I'm trying to impress you," I said, and she smiled. I drank from the beer. The day was hot.

"This is very good," she said.

"Thanks. Do you want another one of these?" I asked her.

"I'm okay," she said. "This is still full."

"I'm drinking too quick."

"Nice day for it," she said.

"It is."

She asked me something about work, and I told her something, just talking, saying anything. I was wondering when Alex was going to arrive and get me out of this.

But what was wrong with me? The two of us lay there with the smell of grass and trees and earth, drinking beer. She was beside me, happy enough, and the only thing that was making it difficult was my inability to accept it. My life could be like this. It was like this. Let Alex come when he wanted. I was okay. I could feel the tightness across my forehead as the beer began to take effect in the warmth of the day, and I knew that a wave of goodwill would be following shortly. I lay back and stared up at the sky for a few minutes. My head was parallel with her legs and when I turned my head to see where she was, I realized I was looking straight up her skirt. It wasn't deliberate, I hadn't tried to get myself in this position. Even by accident it didn't seem fair, though. I laughed at myself, at my private moment of doubt, the things that I would nearly do. Huge white clouds were inching across the sky, connected by the fat fading lines of plane trails.

"What's funny?" she said.

"This is just great," I said.

"It's nice. It was a good idea to come."

"I have very good ideas."

"Are you getting drunk already?"

"I've got a bit of a buzz," I said. "It's the sun."

"And an empty stomach."

"Have you forgotten the lunch I gave you? Already?"

"You didn't eat much of it. You gave most of it to me."

"I'm happy you noticed."

"I noticed."

I lay there feeling warm. If everything had stayed like this forever, it would have been enough for me.

"So why didn't you want to meet up with Fiona?" she said then out of nowhere. I burst out laughing. The cheek of her, taking advantage of my happiness, of the day that we were having.

"Jesus Christ," I said. "Can we not just relax?"

"I am relaxed," she said. "I'm just asking you. What was the problem?"

I sighed.

"There was no problem."

"Did you not like her?"

"No. That wasn't it at all. Why would you think that?"

"Because you didn't want to go out that night with us."

"That doesn't mean that I didn't like her."

"It's one possibility. It's not a problem, David. You don't have to like everybody."

"I know that. But I don't dislike Fiona."

"You're not interested in her, though. You don't fancy her."

"I don't know, Jesus." I leaned over and took another beer out of the bag. "You're something else," I said. "What makes you think you can ask me about this? Am I not allowed to have a bit of mystery in my life? You can't expect me to tell you everything." I could talk to her like this with drink. It might change things. I was aware of that as I spoke.

"I just thought, you know. How often do we get to talk on our own? How many times without Alex around the place making up our little triangle? When is it just you and me?" She was looking at me, an expression on her face that I couldn't read. I wanted to say something sharp back to her, but her using the word *triangle* had thrown me. I didn't react.

"Just you and me? Never," I said. "Or hardly ever."

"So then? Tell me."

"What?"

"Why didn't you want to meet her again?"

I shook my head.

"She's very nice. You know that."

"Sure," she said.

"And I had a good time with her that night we met up, that second time. I liked her, really I did."

"Okay. But?"

I didn't know what to say. I sat looking at her and then eventually spoke.

"I'm kind of interested in someone else."

"Are you?" she said. She sat up and looked at me with interest. "Are you really? Alex doesn't know about this."

"I don't tell him everything."

"So who is she? What's her name?"

"I don't know."

"Well, if you don't, who does?"

"Sorry?" I was confused, trying to regroup. Trying to think what I could say and what I shouldn't. Hoping that my lies wouldn't trip me up. "I didn't mean to tell you this," I said to her then.

"Why not? Who is she?"

"You don't know her. She's a girl in work."

"And why didn't you tell us?" she asked me.

"Because it's nothing. There's nothing to tell."

"There obviously is. Look at you." She reached over and ran her hand across my face. It didn't seem like something she should be doing.

"She's with somebody else, and nothing's going to come of it," I said.

"Do you love her?"

"Yes," I said. Given that I'd chosen to head down this road, why not?

"And has she been with this other guy for long?"

"Not really."

"Could you tell her?"

"No."

"Why not?"

"Because I can't. Because I don't know if she's interested in me at all, and it could mess everything up."

"But if you love her . . ."

"If I love her what?"

"You should say. Be honest."

"No," I said. "You're wrong. That's not a good idea."

"Why not?"

"Because I can't. There's too much involved, and she's with somebody else, and that's all there is to it. I'm telling you. It's not the right thing to do."

"Does anybody know about this?"

"You do."

She was looking at me now.

"You're a dark horse," she said.

"Yeah," I said. "Full of secrets." As I stared at her and she looked away, I thought in that moment that she knew. Just something in the way she turned in on herself and said nothing. I lay back and listened to my heart thump in my ears.

"Other people and their complications," I said after a minute. "Who needs them?"

"We all do," she said.

Lying here. Lying. All the time. The truth was something that could devastate my world, make it all fall apart, end my oldest friendship, drive her away from me, leave me with nothing. What would she do if I sat up now and told her? If I stopped staring up into the sky, broke free from everything that terrified me, and came out with it all? One sentence. It didn't need to be complicated. I love you. That would be all. What would happen? I sat up, felt the head rush, and leaned forward on my knees. She was faced away from me. I felt the words come as far as my throat, rising like something that was going to come out, but then I stopped them. Say something, I thought. Just see if anything will come. She looked at me now and smiled.

"Are you all right?" she said, and it seemed like the easiest thing to reach out and touch her. Hold her hand and say nothing, forget about the words that had never worked for me anyway. Easier to say nothing, easier to do. She was right there, inches away from me, and I could do it. I knew in that instant that if I did, it would go my way. I would hold her hand and she would look at me and I would lean over and the two of us would kiss here in the middle of nowhere in a space that would belong to us forever, with the grass and the blossom on the hawthorn and the bees buzzing and the birds singing and the happy exotic people in the planes miles above us looking down and seeing it all. Seeing us. It was there to be done. I looked at her, and she knew it too. I could tell.

"What is it?" she said.

"Hello," I said.

"I don't think Alex is coming."

"Maybe not."

"Should I give him a ring?" This was going to be it. It was going to be a choice made by me. I could say no. No, don't call him. We don't need him. It's not about him. Everything is here. I could have said any of this, anything would have done. She was waiting for me, the two of us staring at each other. I thought of him. What would he do in this situation? I thought I knew, but still I couldn't do it.

"Call him," I said. "See what's happened."

She looked at me for a second.

"I should really, shouldn't I?" Was she trying to punish me, or did she even know?

"Ring him," I said, standing up. "We can meet him in town if he's still there." She got her phone out and made the call as I started packing up.

"Hi," she said. "Where are you? Okay. We'll come in and meet you. See you soon. Bye."

"He's still there?"

"Yeah."

"They always go on longer than they're supposed to," I said.

"You'd think he'd consider that," she said, "before he starts making arrangements. He's done this to me before."

"Yeah," I said. "I don't know."

We walked back across the fields in silence. We didn't talk when we were loading up the car or on the way back into town. She parked on a square near where he was working. We walked along until we saw the vans and the roadblocks, all the people standing around.

"All this for a twenty-second ad," she said, and I nodded, not looking at her. We walked to where the lights were on and saw him, standing in a group of people looking into a monitor. She went up behind him and touched him on the shoulder.

"Hello," he said. "You're here."

"Are you nearly finished?" she asked.

"Yeah. Pretty much. I'm really sorry. I just couldn't get away. What's the plan?"

She looked at me. I should have done what I wanted when I had the chance. It was gone now. Next time. Next time. I shrugged, and she smiled at me, a sad little pout.

"Well, I need to eat," he said. "I haven't eaten all day."

"I thought they had food at these things," I said. I didn't know that I thought it until I said it.

"No," he said. "The caterers never showed." She laughed at nothing, took a step closer to him, relaxing now that they were back together. If she had felt something, any little guilty frisson, it was over. She was back where she was always meant to be, and everything that had gone before was disappearing fast.

"So will we do that? Get something to eat and then go for a drink or something? Somewhere outside?" The two of them were looking at me.

"No," I said. "I'm going to go."

"Where?"

"Home. I've had enough outside for today. Ask her." I could hear myself. I sounded rude. Too bitter.

"It was great," she said. "We were in this place in the park. Do you know it?"

"Where?"

"I don't know. David found it."

"He's never taken me," Alex said. "Why is that?"

I had to say something.

"I don't know. Maybe next time. Anyway. Have a good night. I'll talk to you soon."

"You're sure? You're going to go?"

"Yeah. I'll give you a call during the week." I was moving away from them when she came over to me and hugged me. I could smell her, feel the warmth of the day's sun coming out of her bones. She kissed me quickly.

"Thank you," she said. "I had a great time."

"It was nice."

"It was." She was holding my hand. I could feel him looking at the two of us and tried to imagine his expression. I wondered whether he had more of an idea of what was going on than I did. I broke away from her, gave him a little wave, and walked off without looking back at the two of them together, the bag of rubbish and empty bottles clinking against my leg. How could I have believed, I wondered then, that the day would end any other way?

CHAPTER ELEVEN

Alex rang me at nine o'clock on a Saturday night. I was on the couch asleep in front of the TV, going nowhere. I hadn't seen him in a while, he'd been picking up work on shoots around town. I thought he'd want to chat, but he was all business.

"What are you doing now?" he asked.

"Nothing."

"Right," he said. "Here, do you want to go bowling?"

I laughed.

"Why would I want to do that?"

"Because Camille's got a friend in town, and that's what she fucking well wants to do. There's four half-drunk girls and me going bowling."

"I don't think so. It's not really my thing."

"Jesus. It's not my thing either. I was supposed to be

meeting people in town, and now she's landed this on me. I don't have a choice."

"Yes, but I do. And I really don't want to go."

"Oh, come on. Do me a favor."

I waited for a second, trying to judge it.

"You're not trying to set me up or anything?"

"No. Though I'll tell you, they've been drinking since five. They're all happy and giggling. A lot of guys would see this as an opportunity."

"So why don't you ring one of them?"

He sighed.

"Because they're all busy on a Saturday night."

"And then you thought of me?"

"Please. I'll pick you up. I'll pay for you."

"Okay. When will you be here?"

"I'm outside," he said. "We better get moving."

We went back and got Camille and her friends from her house. They were getting stuck into a mix of vodka and rum and juice that didn't look clever. They were a wall of noise, all shouting to be heard and laughing and filling each other in. We got into the car and drove out the motorway to a bowling alley. I was in the back with some girl I didn't know on my lap. Once I realized that I had no role to play in the evening, I relaxed. I didn't mind just going with it and letting it all wash over me. Alex was getting edgier. He drove, and nobody listened when he asked for directions. They didn't hear him, and I couldn't help laughing. His job was delivery. Facilitating these girls on a night that was all about them. It didn't suit him.

I hadn't been in a bowling alley for years. It was the same as I remembered it, the same feeling that everybody there was compromising themselves in some way. Sticky carpets. Other people's shoes. No drink. The awkward rangy kids who were old enough to go out but not to get into pubs had to settle for this, cruising each other in groups, all pretending that they were waiting for somebody more interesting. The families doing something together to prove that they could, full of suppressed resentment. The couples who must have had some enormous trauma in their lives to be doing this on a Saturday night.

And then there were the other groups like us, drunk and ironic, but beginning to realize that this wasn't going to be as funny as they'd thought, regretting now that they'd paid for two hours in advance.

We all played on one lane. The girls started, and Alex and I went last. There was a lot of confusion, whose go it was, whose ball was whose, how the scoring worked, and every minute that went by Alex's entire body seemed to tighten like a fist.

"What's the problem?" I asked him as he stood there, chewing his lip.

"This is my Saturday night," he said. "Babysitting a bunch of girls at a bowling alley."

"We can get a drink or something later."

"I could be doing that right now."

"But you're here, so what's the point in getting annoyed about it? Just relax and enjoy it."

"What's wrong with him?" Camille asked me, coming over, all buzzed and smiley.

"He's complaining," I said. "He's not happy."

"Nothing new there."

"You're okay?" he said to her. "Not too drunk? Not laughing too hard?"

"What's wrong with you?"

"What?"

"You're being obnoxious."

"I'm fine," he said. "You just enjoy yourself." He went off to take his go. Camille and I stood beside each other in silence and watched as he hurled a ball straight into the gutter.

"You're not even trying," I shouted at him.

"Fuck off, David," he called back. He wandered off to a Coke machine.

"Fuck off?" I called after him.

"Why is he being like this?" Camille asked me.

"He'll be all right," I said with no conviction in my voice.

"I don't know," she said, still watching him. "What am I going to do with him?" She rested her head on my shoulder. I didn't move, just waited, the two of us standing leaning into each other. When he came back and saw her there, he pretended to smile to himself.

I went and took my go. There was a cheer in the background. I went and stood beside Alex.

"Did you see that?"

"What?"

"I knocked them all down or whatever. What's that called again?"

"A strike," he said. "Well done."

"Thanks."

"Another skill for your résumé."

I looked at him. He stared straight ahead.

"What is your problem?"

"What?"

"You're being rude," I said.

He laughed in a way that made me hope for a second that it had been a joke.

"You're the only person I know under seventy who would use the word *rude*," he said then.

"Oh, shut up," I said then. "Why did you ask me here?"

"Because I thought you might make it more bearable. I didn't know you'd be as bad as the rest of them."

"What? Having fun?"

"Doing a fucking sympathy number on Camille."

"I wasn't," I said.

"It's your turn," one of the girls said to him. He went up. I could see that this time he was trying, but still it was a disaster. On my next go I got another strike. More cheers. I was good at this. Across the room I saw him talking on the phone.

It was a bad idea to have come. Whatever was eating him was beginning to threaten the whole stability of the night. She was okay. Her friends were around her, seemingly oblivious to what was going on. He came over to me, his jacket in his hand.

"I'm off," he said.

"Now?"

"Yeah, I'm meeting Patrick in town."

"You're going to go in the middle of this?"

"Yeah, but look at them. They don't need me." We watched the girls, happy and loud.

"Is this because I'm better at bowling than you?"

"No," he said. "What the fuck does that mean? You're not anyway."

"I was joking," I said.

"I don't care about bowling. I'm bored and pissed off, and I've got to get out of here."

"Okay. Well, you better tell Camille."

"I know I have to tell her. You don't have to give me lessons on etiquette. I know what I have to do."

"Have I done something to annoy you?" He looked at me as if he was going to say something, then stopped himself. "What's wrong with you?" I asked.

"Why are you always here?"

"I haven't been here in years."

"I don't mean this place. I mean with us. Hanging around all the time."

"You invited me. Jesus."

"Yeah, and you came."

"What was I supposed to do? I didn't know it was a problem." He sighed and shook his head.

"It's not," he said. "I'm sorry. I'm just hassled. With everything."

"I don't know what that means. What are you talking about? Tell me."

"I can't. Do you not understand that? It's got nothing to do with you."

"Then why did you get me involved?"

"I don't know," he said. He shrugged. "Do you need a lift home?"

"No," I said.

"Right. I'll see you around."

I watched as he went over to Camille and spoke to her. I saw a flash of disappointment or anger cross her face, I couldn't tell which, before she nodded and smiled. It was a cold nothing of a smile that was for the benefit of anybody watching. She turned from him, and at the point where her eyes met mine, I looked away. I didn't know what I should do, or if I should do anything. She didn't seem like the kind of girl who would take shit from a boyfriend. But then what did I know? It could be different when she was on her own with him. Whatever the truth of it, being there in between the two of them all the time was doing me no good.

I HAD THREE MONTHS before the new job would start, and nothing else that was keeping me there. On the Monday of the following week I went to the bank and spoke to a manager. He looked at my statements and listened to what I had to say about my prospects and qualifications, his head bobbing with enthusiasm as if I had a monopoly on good sense. He kept nodding even when I told him how much I needed.

"Where are you going to go?" he asked at the end, when it was clear that I would be getting my loan.

"Brazil," I said, as if I'd decided.

"Why wouldn't you?" he muttered as he sat forward and started tapping the money through the ether over to my account.

I talked to O'Toole, and he said it was a good idea. He said once I was back by the start of October, then he would be happy. I gave my notice and worked out my final week in the bank with no sense of regret.

I toyed with the idea of leaving without speaking to Alex but in the end I couldn't. It seemed like too big a thing to do.

"Where?" he said when I told him.

"You heard me."

"Are you messing?"

"No. Why would I be?"

"Because they will eat you."

"Who will?"

"Everybody. A child like you has no business in a place like that."

"You've never been there. What do you know?"

He stopped and sighed.

"You'll have to be careful."

"I know that."

"On your own in Brazil."

"Yes."

"Jesus. Why are you doing this?"

I said nothing for a moment, but if he thought about it at all, he might have been able to guess.

"It will be good for me," I said.

"It might be. If they don't catch you."

"They won't catch me," I said, and then he laughed.

I met Camille in a café. She said she wanted to see me before I went when I called her. She asked me everything about where I would go and what I would do. She spoke to me without looking, smiling at me occasionally, little flashes of herself that only showed up how much was wrong.

"Are you all right?" I asked her in the end.

"I'm fine."

"You don't seem it."

"No. I'm okay." She sat stirring the cup in front of her.

"Tell," I said. "You have to now. I'm going away. I won't be here when you decide you want to talk."

She tried to smile at me.

"That friend of yours," she said then.

"What about him?"

"I know it's hard for you," she said. I laughed before I could stop myself. A short little bark. She didn't seem to notice. "Does he tell you anything?" I shook my head.

"Not really. I haven't seen much of him recently."

"Me neither. What's he up to?"

"I don't know," I said after a second.

"He says he's working all the time. He is. I know he is."

"He seems to be."

"I'm sorry to do this to you," she said then. "It's not fair. But I thought if there was something he was worried about, he might have told you. That's all, I promise you. I'm not looking for you to tell me anything you shouldn't. Just has he said anything? Do you think he's all right? Should I be worried about him?"

"I don't know," I said.

"Is it all right me asking you this?"

"It's fine. But I can't tell you anything. Maybe he's having a tough time at work. Maybe he's fighting with his flatmates or his parents. I know he was worried about going back to college, but he hasn't told me anything recently." She was looking at me now, staring straight into my eyes, but she wasn't finding what she wanted. "Ask him," I said. "He'll let you know if there is something wrong."

"I have asked him. He says it's nothing."

"Then maybe it is."

"And he's been okay with you? Normal?"

I shrugged.

"Normal? Yeah, I suppose so."

"Is this why you're going away?" she asked me then. "To get away from us? From all of this?"

"No," I said. "Why would you think that?"

"I don't know. It can't be much fun watching this going on. I wouldn't blame you."

"That's not it at all," I said. "I do have a life of my own. I'm going away for fun, and because I won't get another chance for a while."

"Yeah, I know," she said vaguely, but her mind had already drifted back to him.

CHAPTER TWELVE

I slept in the lower bunk of a bed for ten hours. It was half past nine when I woke. There were no windows in the room, and I lay there not knowing where I was, trying to work out if it was day or night. I could hear the echo of talk in the hall outside. I got up and walked out into the darkness. The thick air smelled of exhaust and drains and fruit beginning to turn. I walked across the park in front of the hostel. There was nobody around, but there was noise everywhere, the sound of televisions from the apartments above, music from the bar on the far side of the square. The crackle and screaming of mopeds driven by bare-chested boys, girls in shorts and tank tops on the back. Beneath it all, in the moments when the noise dropped, I could hear the shushing roaring hum that was a city full of traffic and people, with the sea breaking somewhere in the background. I went into the bar. It was open to the street, a line of guys in blue shirts at the counter, some standing, some sitting on stools around a table in a group, like they were all at the end of a shift. There was a woman on her own, drunk and swaying and talking to the room in general, but nobody paid her any attention. They were all drinking beer out of bottles and frosted glasses, and it was loud. I stood at the counter. Nobody looked at me. The barman was at the far end smoking and talking to an old fellow. I stared over, and when he looked back up the bar at me, I nodded at him. He didn't move. I could feel my face get hot, but still nobody seemed to notice me. Farther down the bar a guy slapped the counter a couple of times.

"Oi," he shouted. "Oi." The barman walked down to him, asked what he wanted, and got it for him from a fridge. As he was walking by me, I stuck out my hand.

"Hey," I said. He stopped and looked at me. I asked him for a beer. One word. He said something back. I shrugged and pointed at a bottle the man beside me was drinking. He brought the same thing to me and I paid, giving him a note that had to be enough. There was a television behind the bar mounted on a wall, and there was a news program on. There were clips, footage of bus crashes and car pileups and other scenes of mayhem, broken bodies lying in bloody heaps. I drank and looked at the screen while around me people had conversations along the length of the bar. All shouting and ar-guing and laughing. When they needed him, they summoned the barman, by whistling, shouting, clicking their fingers. The woman came and stood in front of me saying something. I looked at her and smiled, turned away. She smiled back and reached forward and touched my face. She spoke to me again. The guy beside me laughed and spoke to me and took hold of my arm. He pointed at her, and the two of them started talking at the same time.

"Don't understand," I said. He was laughing at me now. She walked off, and he punched me on the shoulder, playing, and spoke into my face slowly.

"No," I said. "Sorry." His humor seemed to be on the brink of turning into something else. I picked up my bottle and finished it. I walked out. He shouted after me, and I didn't look back. I crossed to the hostel, back into my room with no window, and turned on the fan. I lay there on the bed and tried to remember what it was that I was doing there.

When I woke in the morning, my first morning, there was a guy sitting on the bunk opposite looking at me. He was wearing a tank top and shorts and flip-flops, blond hair cut short.

"Hey," he said. I was trying to remember where I was, how I'd got there, if I was supposed to know this person.

"Hello," I said, sitting up, becoming aware of the fact that I was in my underwear.

"Did you just arrive?"

"Yesterday. Yeah."

"You slept a long time. Are you English?"

"Irish. Are you American?"

"Canadian."

"Sorry," I said. "Just the accent."

"Yeah. I know. Me too. Do you want to go and eat something?"

"Okay. I'll need ten minutes."

"I'll wait for you out front. What's your name, by the way?"

"David."

"I'm Dirk," he said.

"Dirk," I repeated. "All right."

I was trying to work out what he wanted when I was having a shower. The most benign thing I could come up with was that he was on his own and was lonely. I wondered why that would be, what could be wrong with him that he would be here on his own, like me.

"How long will you will be here?" he asked me as we were walking down a dark narrow street toward the sea, a blue burst of color and light visible ahead.

"A couple of months. I was going to go down to Argentina after a while."

He shrugged.

"That could be fun, I suppose," he said. "But this is better."

"Have you been there?"

"No. But I bet I'm right."

We went into a café that was open onto the street one block away from the beach. An old guy with a cigarette hanging out of his mouth was wiping down a fridge when we sat down. The Canadian pointed at the menu and smiled and the man asked him a couple of questions and he just said yes to everything. We sat at the counter and smoked and watched the guy make juice out of fruit that I didn't recognize.

He was a medical student from Ottawa, and he'd deferred his second year to travel. He arrived here six weeks ago, meaning to go on after a couple of days, but had stayed put.

"Why?" I asked.

"It suits me. That's all. I can't see how anybody couldn't love it. I mean, I don't know you. We've only just met, but don't you get it? Don't you know what I'm talking about?"

"I only got here yesterday. I haven't really seen anything yet. I went for a drink last night."

"And how was that?"

"All right," I said. "Not much fun. Everybody was shouting. I didn't know what was happening."

"That passes," he says. "You just have to get used to it."

"Right," I said. "And how do I do that?"

"Stop worrying. There's nothing to be afraid of. All the trouble is in the hills," he said, waving off into the distance casually as if it were another country. "Down here there's nothing. The cops won't let it. Too many tourists. It's fine, no worse than anywhere. Obviously you have to watch out for yourself. Not be flash or anything. The thing is, it's a very simple life. It's sex and beer and football, and that's it. That's all you need to know. These people are like children. If you can be interested in these things, then you will fit in. And being a foreign boy is like being a girl at home. It's a total reversal. You will get women everywhere coming up to you, whistling at you on the street, touching you in bars. You're not married or engaged or anything. No committed relationship?"

"No," I said.

"Then you will have a very good time. I can show you where to go."

"Okay." He was the only person I could talk to, and he was being friendly, even if he did seem like an idiot. Maybe I just needed to acclimatize like he had. Whistling and doing a squiggle in the air at the old fellow, who produced an ashtray. It felt as if I should respond, so I said something that was true.

"It sounds good."

"You have no idea," he said.

When we finished eating, he asked did I want to go to the beach for the afternoon, but I said I had stuff to sort out. He said he'd see me back in the hostel later. I wandered the streets. People saw me. I could feel myself being watched everywhere, and I didn't like it. They clicked, calling out words at me that I didn't understand. Guys walked along beside me, talking into my ear, telling me things, but when I turned, they skipped away. There was nothing I could do. I just shook my head and kept going.

I went into an Internet café on one of the main streets and sent an e-mail to my parents. I told them that I had arrived and everything was fine. I wrote about what my plans were and where I was going next, even though I didn't know if I would be able to get anywhere. I sat in the window and looked out onto the street. It seemed normal, nothing to be worried about, but I knew that when I went back out there, it would feel different. It wasn't the heat or the fumes or the noise. It was the people and how they would encroach, as if my personal space were an affectation that they meant to rob me of. I wrote an upbeat e-mail to Alex, trying to imagine how I would describe the place if it didn't terrify me. Vibrant. Hot. Sticky. Exciting. I copied it to Camille and sent it. I got back to the hostel and lay on my bed, letting the fan cool my sweat.

CHAPTER THIRTEEN

I woke at seven o'clock that night. There were five or six people in the room talking English, a mix of accents. They were planning a night out. When I opened my eyes and sat up, I saw the Canadian in the middle of them.

"That's David," he said to them. "The cartels didn't get you then."

"Not yet," I said.

"We're going to go into Ipanema. Have some drinks. You want to come?"

"Okay."

There were four of us, all from different places. We went down to the main street to get a bus. It felt better being in a group, being a part of a moving unit of noisy difference. I began to wonder about myself, whether or not I'd just been too tired. I stared back at the people that stared at us as we passed, and nothing happened. They just kept looking, and it didn't escalate into anything bad.

On the street in the warm damp of the night, a breeze coming in from the sea, two hundred people stood around a corner drinking and smoking and eating. There were guys selling beer out of coolers, somebody making caipirinhas out of a bar in the boot of a car, music coming out of the restaurant beside us, and the smell of pizza and perfume and dope. Beautiful people, and we belonged among them because we were from somewhere else. I was sitting on the curb drinking from a can and talking to a Mexican guy when a girl came over and stood above me. She looked like she might be taller than me, dark hair cut in a bob, a black short-sleeved shirt, and a black skirt. She bent over and asked me in English for a light. I went to stand up, but she sat down beside me. I lit her cigarette, and she said, "Do you not like me?"

"What?"

"I've been standing over there for ten minutes, and you didn't come over to me."

"I'm sorry," I said. "I didn't know I was supposed to."

"Only if you like me."

"I like you," I said. I thought this was going well, though I wasn't exactly in control of the situation.

"And I like you," she said, and she stood gazing. Everybody in this country stared at me.

"So," I said. She leaned in, and I kissed her. I wasn't even close to drunk, but it was easy. Eight thousand miles away from home. From my life and its worry and uncertainties and all the agonizing that from here seemed indulgent and pointless and over.

At the end of the night I gave her the number of where I was staying. She said she was working the following morning, so I couldn't come home with her, but she'd call the next day and we could meet and then I could come to her apartment.

"You can stay with me," she said. "For the weekend."

"I'd like that," I said.

I put her in a taxi and went and found the others. As we walked back to the bus stop, Dirk asked me about her, and I told him about her offer.

"She won't call," he said.

"Why not?"

"People here make arrangements all the time just to be friendly. I'll call you. I'll meet you. You must meet my family. It doesn't mean anything. It's just the way they do it."

"Why?"

"Because it's nicer. Everybody's happy. Don't you feel good after talking to her?"

"I did. Until I talked to you."

"She may call," he said, "but I wouldn't hold your breath. And I don't think you should meet her anyway."

"Why not?"

"You can be with a different girl every night here. You don't need to shack up with the first girl you meet."

"Did you see her?" I asked him. "I'm out of my league already."

"It's up to you," he said. "But it is your first day here, man. Your first day."

He patted me on the shoulder and laughed. I thought about punching him, just once in the mouth, but the moment passed.

I wanted her to call to prove him wrong, to show him that he didn't understand this place better than anyone. But when she didn't, and when I thought about it, I didn't mind so much. There was something to it, this idea that people should be told what they want to hear. Everybody was so open about what they wanted that saying no seemed to be rude.

After a couple of days I got used to it. The smell of alcohol and drains, vegetation advancing everywhere as if the city was a temporary arrangement that the plants had agreed to but were now reconsidering. The feeling that if you left the window open in your room, by the time you came back life would have made its way in there and changed things around. Black girls with paler skin than me, German guys driving buses, the beautiful girls who were prostitutes who slowed to check when they saw me, just to see, looking at me yawning just in case I had money and was interested and then turning away, scouting all the time as I looked to the ground. The people who pointed at me and laughed to provoke me. To make me come over and talk. I love you, they shouted. For goodness sake. What time is it?

"Look how this one is nervous," a girl said to her friend as my hand shook, drinking coffee standing at a counter in a café beside them, feeling the warmth as she leaned against me, her back sticking to my damp arm.

"Look," she said, and her friend laughed.

The young rangy guys in shorts and nothing else, barefoot, swaggering in groups as if the streets were theirs and not belonging to the moneymen with linen suits and Italian ties. The lines at juice bars and at the ice cream hatch at McDonald's. The smell of fruit and the undertone of the peelings and waste turning already. Chickens cooking on rotisseries. Dried fish hanging in windows like driftwood. Rice and black beans. Dinner by the hundred grams. Cats and dogs that had torn each other apart. Taxi drivers and cops standing around in groups, and everybody talking the way they did, not like a conversation but like a celebration of the tongue, lips, teeth. A physical demonstration of what you could do with your mouth. The girl who changed my money in the bank who looked like she was trying to kiss me as she bent down to speak English to me through the gap in the glass. The confidence, the ease of their movement. Three homeless guys with Coke bottles of rum, two sitting on the ground, the other lying on the street with his head resting on his hand, having a loud conversation that had been slowed down, the three of them laughing together in coughing, rasping shouts as people walked around them. The cop that took the bottle from one of them and poured it down the drain as the three looked on in sad silence. Shirts you could buy in installments, monthly payments, interest-free. The fight on the street in the middle of the day that sent people running and I froze waiting to see what was going to happen next but then it dissolved, everybody involved melted away and disappeared as the siren grew and the cops arrived at the right place but found nothing. Going to the cinema to get out of the rain on an afternoon, watching a film in English, the only other person being a businessman who made phone calls for the first hour and then slept through the second hour, snoring so insistently that I thought it was a joke.

Passing girls and looking and smiling and, if you liked them, turning to watch them go. It was funny. Dirk told me to walk back after them if I liked the look of somebody. That I should talk to them, and even if they didn't speak English, it wouldn't matter.

During the day we hung around on the beach. There was a group of us from the hostel and then other people turned up. We went out a couple of nights later. I ended up talking to an English guy. He told me about how he had taken out a loan and had spent all his money and his parents sent him a thousand dollars to come home and he was spending that now. He was eighteen. I asked him what he was going to do when that money ran out.

"Get some more. Borrow it. Steal it. I don't know. I may never be here again."

"Yeah, but . . . ," I said.

"Get over yourself," he said. "Not your business."

When we got back to the hostel, I was going to go in with the rest of them, but then I changed my mind. I told Dirk to go on in, said I was going for a walk.

"Be careful," he said.

"Just around this block," I said. I walked down to the corner, not looking for anything, not knowing what I was doing. I was just wandering around in the middle of the night, and I wasn't afraid or worried or thinking about anything.

When I got to the coast road, I turned and walked along, past the tourist bars and the hotels. There was hardly anybody around, just some strip-club bouncers outside places that I couldn't see into. On a corner one block back from the seafront avenue, I saw a bar that was open. A glass-fronted place with a horseshoe-shaped counter. It was busy, a mix of men and women. I went in and ordered a beer. After a minute I realized there was a girl standing beside me, and she wanted me to talk to her. She was on her own, facing the other way, but she was standing so close to me, I could feel the warmth of her arm against mine. It wasn't that crowded. I said hello in Portuguese, and she spoke back to me in English. I bought her a drink, and she asked me where I was from, and we talked about that for a while. As I was finishing my beer, she put her arm around my neck and pulled me close to her.

"Come on," she said into my ear. "Let's get out of here."

We walked out hand in hand back down to the coast road. She walked straight on across the avenue onto the sweeping black-and-white wave mosaics beside the beach.

"Where are we going?" I asked her.

"Down here," she said.

"Where?"

"In the sand. You will love it." She broke away and ran on ahead of me. I followed, picked up my pace to try and catch her. She turned around and laughed and I ran after her and then I tripped and landed on my face in the sand. I was thinking that I didn't know why I'd fallen, and then there was somebody on my back, a hand on my head pushing it down into the sand. One of my arms was bent around and pulled up behind me, hurting but ready to hurt more. There were two of them, I realized now, and there was something hard being pushed into the back of my neck, something cold and metal. I could hear them panting, could feel the breath of one of them as he leaned in close to my face, a sweet alcoholic smell. He spoke to me slowly, sounding calm.

"I don't understand," I said. "No Portuguese."

"Money?" he said then.

I felt hands going through my pockets, patting down my legs. My shoes were pulled off. "There's no more," I said. I needed them to know. I felt them move, the pressure lifted off me.

"Now. You don't move."

I lay there for a minute or two as I heard them run off. I could feel my heart beating. I lifted my head, then turned around and saw that I was alone, nobody, just waves lapping at the shore and the lights of the hotels behind. The dark of the Sugarloaf was ahead of me. It was very beautiful. I stood up slowly and walked back up to the road. I went up to two bouncers in black T-shirts. I saw them looking at my feet before I spoke.

"They robbed me," I said. One of them said something back, the other shook his head and shrugged. They started talking to each other and turned away from me, just a shade of an angle that told me I should move on. I walked back in the direction of the hotels. A police car came along the seafront, and I put my hand up. The car slowed and stopped beyond me. Two guys got out quickly and walked over, not looking at me, watching up and down the road.

"Speak English?" I said to the first one as he came up and stood beside me. He was one step too close.

"What do you want?"

"Two guys on the beach. They robbed me. Just now." He still wasn't looking at me. His hand was resting on his gun as I spoke. I could only see the other guy out of the corner of my eye. I tried not to move.

"On the beach?"

"Yes."

"Why were you on the beach?"

"Why? I don't know."

"You buy drugs? Or went with a girl or a boy?"

"No drugs. No. Nothing."

"So why do you go to the beach? You didn't see the signs?"

"What signs?" He translated back to his colleague, and the two of them laughed. I spoke slowly.

"I met a girl in the bar back along there," I said, "and we went on the beach and then she ran off and two guys came and robbed me. They put me on the ground and took my money and my shoes. That's all."

"There was a girl?"

"Yes."

"Did you pay her?"

"No. No."

"Why did you go to the beach?"

"I don't know," I said. "I thought . . . I don't know why." The two of them laughed again.

"You know why. I know why. How much did they take from you?"

"Thirty dollars. Maybe forty."

"You are lucky." He walked back to the car. I stood with the other guy, and the two of us stared out across the road at the sea, the beach hidden by darkness. When the other guy came back, he handed me a notebook.

"Write your name and country here." I did it and handed the book back to him. He copied something down, and then gave me a card. "Come to this address tomorrow at two o'clock and ask for this man. He will take a report. Okay?"

"Okay," I said.

"Do not go onto this beach at night. They can kill you. Don't come back here. Do you know where you are?"

"Yes."

"So go home. You have a hotel?"

"A hostel."

"Okay."

I stood looking at him and nodded.

"Thank you," I said.

"Go," he said, shaking his hand at me. "Go home."

I walked back barefoot, picking my way through broken glass and rubbish and every type of shit on the street. By the time I got to the square, the familiar smell and light of a space that seemed like my own, I had started to feel something like euphoria. I had been mugged. It hadn't hurt. I hadn't lost anything important. I wasn't afraid. In a situation where other people might have done the wrong thing, shouted or panicked or fought back in some way, not because it mattered to them but because that would be how they would react, I had done the right thing. I had put myself in danger through my own stupidity, but I had known what to do to get out of it. I had survived.

The following afternoon I sat on a bench in a room in a police station, holding the card that the policeman had given me the previous night. The door to an office was across from me, a removable plaque with four names slotted into it on the wall beside it. Every few minutes people would cross the room, carrying files. None of them looked at me as they passed. I had been directed to this room when I arrived, had knocked on the door, but nobody answered. I didn't know what to do, so I sat. At half past two a man went into the office. Indian looking, goatee, long hair in a ponytail down his back, gun in a holster on his belt. He closed the door behind him. I got up and went over. I could hear him talking inside, maybe on the phone. I knocked on the door and waited. Nothing happened. I waited until he stopped talking, and then I knocked again. Nothing. I began to think that maybe there was another door in the room that led on to somewhere else. I sat down again and waited. I had only come because the guy the night before had taken my name. What could they do? Give me forty dollars? Take me shopping for shoes? I didn't want to be there, and now I didn't know what to do. So I did nothing. I sat on the bench and waited for something to happen. At a quarter to five, the same guy came out of the office. He locked the door behind him. I stood up.

"Senhor Oliveira?"

"Yeah?"

He turned to me and I saw that he was ready for an argument. He wasn't happy.

"I was told to come here." I handed him the card. "I was robbed last night." He looked at the card for long enough that I felt I should say something else. As I was about to speak, he held the card in front of my face, pointing at it.

"What time does this say?"

"Two o'clock."

"And now it's . . . ?"

"A quarter to five."

"So?"

"I was there," I said, pointing at the seat.

"You were there. You were there. So what if you were there?"

"I knocked on the door."

"When?"

"When you arrived."

His voice was getting louder.

"Why didn't you speak to me? Why didn't you say something?" He had more to tell me, but he stopped. Then started again. This time in Portuguese.

"I didn't know it was you," I said, but he kept shouting, getting louder all the time. I said it again, trying to make him hear me, but I didn't even know what I was saying anymore. He wasn't listening, and I couldn't understand him. I knew that he was wrong to be getting so annoyed, that he should let me explain, but he wouldn't. I wouldn't stand there and be shouted at.

"You're a bad policeman," I said at him, and it disappeared into the confusion of two languages being shouted at the same time. Then I said it again. This time he stopped.

"What did you say?"

"I said you're a bad policeman." We stood maybe a foot apart, facing each other. He was the same height as me, heavier build. He had a gun on his hip, and in the silence I became very aware of that fact. It was not a clever thing to have said. He could have done anything. He laughed out loud, and I thought I was in real trouble. But then he slapped me on the shoulder and took the keys out of his pocket. We went into the office, and he sat behind his desk. He offered me a cigarette, and the two of us smoked as I told him what had happened and he typed it up. When I left he shook my hand, still chortling away to himself, and I walked off, still shaking.

A crowd of us went to the same place in Ipanema. I sat on the curb talking to a girl, an American in the middle of a six-month trip. She was half drunk and obviously hadn't spoken to anyone for a while. She talked to me about television, food, the things that were going on around us. I looked at her face as she spoke. She had a scar that curved in a C on her top lip, which seemed to make what she said more thoughtful. When she looked at me to emphasize a point, she touched it with a quick familiar movement and turned away. She was telling me what her life was like back in Minnesota. The steamy buzzing summers with sprinklers in the day and crickets at night, flat low suburbs with space everywhere, in between the houses, between the gardens and the roads, the pools and the decks, as if they had to use it up. The cool supermarkets that smelled of coffee and cinnamon, the misting sprays that made the fruit and vegetables shiny and too beautiful to disturb, too elegant to eat. The old women on the tills, their hair piled up on their heads, Scandinavian and Irish and German names on their tags. Anderson. O'Neill. Schmidt. She told me about the winter, the first snows that came in October and stayed until April. The city center joined together by heated corridors three stories up, the streets beneath empty of people. The breath that froze in your nose, the crackle of the fur on your hood, the days off school when it got below minus twenty.

"It sounds amazing," I said.

"It's not, really. I just miss it. I'm sure where you're from is just as interesting."

I laughed.

"I don't think so."

"Why? What's wrong with it?"

"Nothing. It's just damp and gray and complicated."

"How so?"

"I don't know," I said. "I haven't been thinking about it very much."

We sat on the pavement of a street that was blocked off, drinking beer from cans and smoking on an evening that was so warm and damp and airless it was like being inside an animal. She talked about her family and a guy with whom she'd broken up a week before she'd left. What a prick he was, she told me, but if he'd appeared suddenly beside her now, I thought she would have thrown him to the ground and straddled him.

"What about you?" she asked after a while to be polite. "What do you do?"

"I'm a musician," I said.

"Really?"

"Yeah. Why not?" And she laughed, confused.

"Cool."

They all went on somewhere else, some club that would go till morning. I left them on the street, hugging people I'd never spoken to, shaking hands. I kissed the American girl on the mouth, just quickly, to show her that we were closer, and she laughed. I had seventy-five cents in my fist and a couple of notes in the pocket of my shorts. The bus came, and I dropped the money in the slot, walked through the turnstile. We went into the darkness of a tunnel, and when we came out, two guys got on, young fellows, skinny, muscled, flexed. They jumped the barrier, and the driver didn't even turn. They came back and sat across the aisle a couple of seats ahead of me, one behind the other, and draped themselves across the benches. Their voices were too loud. When they turned back to look at me, I dropped my eyes and then stared out the window at the shops and restaurants flying by, the newspaper and rubbish blowing in the breeze that was coming up from the sea, the curled-up bodies lying asleep in doorways. In the glass of the window I watched the reflection of the two boys as they looked at me in a moment of silence and then turned away.

The following day I went back to the Internet café. I was trying to find out where I wanted to go next. There was an island just off the coast down south. I checked my e-mail. There was a message from my father, saying that he hoped I was getting on well and that if I needed money to let him know.

"Do not hesitate," he said. "Do not be embarrassed."

And there was one from Camille. She said, "It was lovely

to hear from you. Glad everything is going well and I wish I was there. You are missed. Get home safe. Love C xxx."

I read it again and couldn't understand why what she had written thrilled me as much as it did. I tried to remember what it was that had driven me away from a situation that had surely been moving toward some kind of resolution. That escalating tension had been there for a reason. From here it seemed much clearer. When I went back, things would be different. I would tell her everything. There was nothing to be afraid of, no embarrassment about how I felt, no moral dilemma in acting on it. Alex had known all along that I loved her, and he hadn't let that fact hold him back. He was a friend, but he'd been wrong. It was simple. I closed the window on the computer and got up to go. A shiver passed through me, a flash of doubt that I felt in my stomach, but I wouldn't let it take hold. Uncertainty was like a habit. I sighed and distracted myself by thinking of the next place I had to go.

I traveled by bus for two days, trying to sleep the whole way, leaning against a window as people beside me came and went. I woke at various points and saw what was going on. I watched São Paolo beneath us as we went up a motorway on the side of a hill, spreading farther than I could see, as if the whole of the country was covered in orange lights. The other people on for the whole trip started to nod at me and smile. When we went into garages, we would stand on the forecourt beside our bus having three-word conversations and smoking. I am tired. Give me fire. You want drink? I saw how people on the bus arranged themselves in the seats in the most comfortable way possible, propping each other up, wrapping themselves around their neighbors even if they were strangers. I half-woke when a woman got on at three o'clock one of the mornings and straightened myself up to give her room, but then she put her head on my shoulder and fell asleep. I tried not to move, but when I woke two hours later she was asleep in my lap and I had my arm across her waist.

On the boat out to the island we bounced along, the bags piled at the back getting wetter with each fall. Nobody seemed to care. It was a Friday, I realized then; the others there were down from the cities for the weekend, and you could tell that they were already unwound, laughing at the hopping and the waves, oohing and aahing when we rocked too heavy, and I began to wonder, but their laughter brought me back from worry.

"I like England," the girl sitting beside me said.

"Do you speak English?" I asked her, and she nodded. "Is this a good island?" I said then. She shrugged.

"What's your name?" She didn't know what I was talking about.

When we arrived and hopped up onto the rickety jetty, I had no plan. I had picked the island out of a guidebook because they said it was quiet and a place to relax and I was ready for that after forty-eight hours on a bus. As soon as I walked onto the beach, a guy came up alongside me. A mover, about thirty. He spoke to me without looking.

"What you need? What you want? You have hotel?"

I was going to walk away, but I had no idea where I was going, so I said yeah. We walked together along the sand, and he said nothing.

"How much?" I asked him then.

"What do you want to pay?" he said.

I told him a price that was too low.

"Okay," he said. "Here."

We turned off the beach and walked up a path through the trees. I looked around. A wide flat beach with nobody on it, green hills rising out of the water ahead. There was no sign of any of the people that had come over with me. I followed the guy up, and he went into a house at the side of a dirt road. It smelled of cooking, and I could hear a baby crying. He called out as we walked in, and a girl stuck her head around the door.

"Oi," she said. He brought me up to a room. A spare room. There was a cot and a computer on a desk.

"When are you going?" he asked me.

"Three days?" I said.

"Okay. If you want to eat, tell us," and then he was gone. I got into the bed, and when I woke up it was Saturday afternoon.

IN A HALL BESIDE a scrubby football pitch in the middle of the island there were three hundred people gathered dancing. Everybody was there. Outside the air was cloudy with smoke from a barbecue and buzzed with the noise of generators. Speakers pumped out music in the four corners of a space that had a corrugated roof and only one wall. There was a bar at one end, and I stood at that, drinking beer. I was watching the crowd move in unison, bouncing together and singing a song that went from a recognizable verse into a mad kind of chanting frenzied chorus, the floor shaking as they began to jump again. I found myself on the edge of it all. A woman in her fifties reached over to me and pulled me over to her group.

"I don't know what to do," I said. She said something back to me that I wouldn't have understood even if I had heard it. "You show me," I said, thinking that she didn't know what I was saying, but she did it anyway. She put her arm around me and guided me through the steps, some basic movement tied into a rhythm that she steered me through, our bodies sticking to each other in the heat. She took me out into the middle of them and I had to do it. I had to dance with them, try and do it the way they did. After a while I stopped thinking about it, and it became easier.

CHAPTER FOURTEEN

I thought it would be cold when I got home, but the air was clean and the sun was trying its hardest. The trees on the road were beginning to turn. I went down to my parents' place directly. They were happy to see me. My mother talked about how brown I was and said that I looked well. I slept and had baths and ate from the fridge. I watched television and read papers, and after three days I went back to Dublin. In my own space I began to feel excited about the work that was coming. I allowed myself to imagine what this job would be like, all going well. The things that I would do and what it would take to achieve them.

Alex rang me at home the next day.

"I heard you were back," he said.

"From whom?"

"My mother. She knew before me. Why didn't you call? Is it shit to be home?"

"Not really. Better than I thought. The weather is great."

"The weather. Are you talking to me about the weather?"

"It's nice to hear your voice."

"Did you have fun?"

"It was great. Do you want to hear all about it?"

"If we meet in a pub, I'll happily listen to anything."

"Is Camille around?" He sighed, a little dramatic huff. "What?" I asked.

"I'll find out," he said.

"Is there a problem?"

"Nothing. Just. I have to ring her."

"Yeah. So? I'd like to see her."

"Oh," he said. "Listen to you."

"What?"

"Did you get a bit uppity while you were away? Do you need a beating to sort you out?"

"No," I said. "I'm fine."

As I was about to say good-bye, he spoke again.

"I'm glad you're back," he said.

"Why?"

"I don't know. It'll be good having you around again. I missed you. Your conversational skills, if nothing else."

I met them at a bar in the center of town. I arrived late, and the two of them were already there, sitting outside at a table. They got up when I arrived.

"Look at you," Camille said as she was hugging me. "Welcome back. I missed you."

"And you."

"You've lost weight," she said, patting my sides like I was a horse.

"Maybe a bit."

"You look well," she said, standing back from me.

"So do you."

"Don't mind her," Alex said as he shook my hand and gave me an awkward kind of pat that turned into a near hug. "You look exactly the same. Maybe a little weaker."

We sat, and they asked the questions that they should ask. Where and how and who. I talked for half an hour, but I began to feel embarrassed.

"So what's been going on here? How have you been?"

They looked at each other and kind of smiled.

"Fine. Nothing really going on. I'm back in college," she said.

"And I'm doing bits and pieces."

"But nothing happened? In three months."

"You know what it's like," Alex said. "Working. Sleeping. Out at the weekends. Just normal."

"Right." I looked at him, waiting for him to think of something.

"Hey, you're the one who's been halfway around the world. We just stayed put. Nothing ever happens here."

He looked away down the street, unfocused and unhappy. I wanted to ask him if he was all right, but it was hard with her there. I spoke again before the silence built into something unmanageable.

"I'm glad I went," I said. "But I was happy coming home

when I did. It's good to be starting into something new. And I can go back again. It'll always be there."

"And would you do that?" she asked.

"Maybe. I didn't like it at first. The people are very physical. They touch you and shout and they laugh in your face. It was too much. But then it became normal, and I started doing it too."

"Shouting at people?" Alex said

"No. I mean watching people. Making noise to get the waiter's attention." I banged my fist on the edge of the table and the glasses clinked. Around me people turned and looked.

"Don't do that here," Alex said. "It doesn't work, and people will think you're an arsehole."

"I find myself staring at girls on the street here now," I said. "It's interesting. If you look for even a second longer than you're supposed to, they don't know what to do."

He laughed.

"What?" I asked.

"There's a thin line between seductive and creepy," he said.

"I'm not trying to be seductive," I said. "Just looking. But they notice."

"Maybe they like it," she said.

"Really?" Alex asked her. "Would you? This fucking gimp staring at you in the street?"

She smiled.

"Well, it's different for me. I know him."

"But I've changed now," I said.

"So it seems," she said.

"Did you find yourself?" Alex asked. "In your couple of

months away, did you discover some new truths about who you are?" I looked at him and hesitated. She was staring at him. "What?"

"You're being a dick."

"I'm just messing with him," he said. She shook her head and turned away from him.

"You know everything that's here," I said, touching my chest with my fist. "There's nothing new."

I was glad to leave them after an hour. Alex said he would give me a ring during the week to meet up sometime.

I rang O'Toole on the Monday to let him know I was back around the place if there was anything he needed me to do. Things I should be reading up on.

"You can help do up the office if you're looking for a job," he said. "I'll pay you cash." I laughed. "What's funny?" he asked then.

"I don't know," I said. "I just wasn't expecting you to say that." He cackled to himself. I still wasn't sure if he was serious. "Do you really want me to get involved in this?"

"Yes," he said. "Look, we're setting this up from scratch. The place needs to be decorated and fitted. Stripped out and redone. Get a carpet put in. Straightforward stuff. We won't be starting for a month. I'm not going to sit around and spend a couple of grand watching someone do work I can do myself. It doesn't make sense. I would have thought an enterprising young lad like you would jump at the chance."

"Okay," I said. "I'll do it."

"Hold on now," he said. "Are you any good? Have you experience? References?"

"Not a lot," I said. "No."

"That was a joke. You can meet me there on Wednesday. Wear old clothes."

I sat there trying to work out if this was a normal thing to be doing. It wasn't the start I had imagined. But then if the company was successful, this could become a part of my own legend. I would look back and laugh. If it worked out. The phone rang.

"David?"

"Yes?"

"It's Fred again."

"Fred?"

"Mr. O'Toole, you idiot. Jesus, do you not recognize me? It's only been ten seconds."

"Sorry. I forgot your name was Fred."

"I haven't told you where this place is."

"Oh yeah. Hang on."

"Where were you going to go?" he asked as I was looking around for a pen. I seemed to spend most of our conversations floundering.

"The thought hadn't occurred to me," I said.

"You'll have to do better than that. I'm paying you to think. And to paint. I'll see you on Wednesday."

It was fine for him to talk about how much we would save by doing the work ourselves. After the first day I understood that his role would be as an adviser to me and two of his nephews, tall silent young fellows who never spoke. He wandered around complaining. He talked into his phone and argued with people about chairs and printers and delivery dates and times. He talked with his wife about a holiday that they were going to take before we opened. Intense argument and negotiation with everyone about everything. He'd never paid a penny more for anything than he needed to. After three days of working until after eight o'clock, on the Saturday he took us to the pub at five and bought us pints for a couple of hours. He knew what needed to be done and the order in which to do it. But I never saw him touch a brush.

Alex didn't ring me. The following Wednesday I called him. His phone was off, and I left a message. He texted me back the next day, saying he wanted to meet up. He gave the name of a bar I'd never been in. It was almost ten when we finished work that evening, and I went straight in wearing my dirty clothes, too tired to care. If the bouncers didn't let me in, I wouldn't mind. But there were no bouncers. It was a small old place down a side street, not his sort of thing at all. When I went in, it was packed, and the crowd wasn't what I'd expected either. Good-looking and loud and talking in a way that you'd notice. All very happy. I listened in on snatches of animated conversations as I tried to find Alex. He was standing at the bar, and he smiled when he saw me.

"What the young start-up millionaire is wearing this season."

"He has me painting," I said.

"I can see that. This job not working out the way you'd hoped?"

"I'm happy to be getting paid. What is this place?"

"What do you mean? It's a pub."

"Look around you. Who are these people, and what are they doing in this dump?"

He scanned the room and smiled. "It's not a dump. They're just people. It gets a theater crowd from around the corner, I suppose. Actors and stage crew and the like."

"Actors," I said. "I thought there was something wrong with them. What brings you here?"

"I was at a play earlier. It had its first preview tonight. I was at that, so I just thought it would be a good place to meet. Broaden your horizons."

"I didn't know you did the theater. I thought you were strictly film."

"It overlaps sometimes." He smiled to himself. I bought a round, and we stayed at the counter.

"So where's Camille?" I asked.

"At home." I waited, but he didn't say anything else.

"Not her thing?"

"No, not really."

"And was the play good?"

"It was great. You should see it."

"Sure," I said. "I might do that."

"That means no," he said.

"Not necessarily. So where have you been?" I asked. "I thought we were going to get together last week. I haven't seen you properly since I came back."

"Yeah. I've been busy with work. It's just very unpredictable. I don't know where I'm going to be from one day to the next."

"You could have called."

"Oh, stop whining. I'm here now. We're out together. It's good to see you."

"And you."

"So how come this guy is using you as a decorator?" he asked then. "I thought he said you'd be programming."

We stood at the counter and talked. It was easier than it had been for a long time. Without the distraction of her presence and the tension of being stuck between the two of them, I was relaxed. We knew how to be comfortable around each other, we hadn't forgotten that in a few months. I talked about O'Toole for a while, and he told me then about the jobs he was doing, working for a guy making ads. He was turning up every day on set and doing whatever needed to be done. But it was all experience. Meeting lots of useful people. Making enough money to get by.

It was later on, when we were beginning to loosen up, that I felt it was all right to ask.

"So how is Camille?"

"She's fine." He looked at me and smiled. "You know yourself." I nodded in response, even though I had no idea.

"She seemed in good form," I said.

"When?"

"That day we met in town."

"Oh, yeah," he said. "Actually, I don't think I've seen her since then."

"Seriously? That's nearly two weeks."

"I've been working a lot. Long days."

"Still. She'll have forgotten what you look like."

"David, I don't need you to give me advice—" He cut himself short.

"What?" I said. "Say it."

"I'm sorry," he said. "But I don't want to drag you into my personal life."

"Fair enough," I said, though I was considering how directly involved I'd been since they'd met. I looked around the room, trying to think of something to say, something neutral and dull.

"I haven't been in good form for a while," he said then. "It's hard, you know? We haven't been together that long, so when we're heading in different directions, what are you supposed to do? How much should either of us be prepared to compromise?"

"Are you heading in different directions?"

He said nothing for a moment, maybe deciding how much he wanted to tell me.

"At first she wanted to hang around together all the time, and that was fine. It's the same for everybody when you start. Every day, every night. No problem. But after a while you need to open it up, you know? You need to have your own separate life as well, or you get sick of each other." He saw me react. "Not sick, I don't mean that. I'm just saying you need your own space. You have to get out and work and meet other people and do things. That way when the two of you meet up again, you're happy to see each other. You and me do it. Everybody does. Apart from married people."

"Even some of them," I said.

"Maybe. I don't know. Anyway, once a week I'd plan something that didn't involve her, and she'd do the same, and that was cool. I was happy, she was happy. But then I thought she started getting clingy."

"Clingy," I said. "That doesn't sound like her."

"It probably doesn't. But she'd get pissed off if I arranged things at the weekend that didn't involve her."

"That's hardly clingy," I said.

"I'm not getting into an argument about fucking semantics, David. Just wait a second, will you? Listen to what I'm saying."

"I am listening," I said. "Go on."

"I thought it was clingy. At first. But then I thought, if I'm serious about this girl and if I love her or whatever, I shouldn't just react the same way I always have—back off and stop communicating or act like a prick until she gets bored and wanders off. The fact that a girlfriend wanted to spend time with me at the weekends wasn't unreasonable."

I laughed at that.

"Probably not."

"So I tried to do something," he said. "The whole going-away idea was a part of that. Just the two of us together. We would have been living with each other somewhere new. I wanted to do that with her. I've never done that with anyone else. But she pissed me off, stalling until it wasn't an option and then telling me that maybe I should stay here and finish college. She didn't see what it was that I was saying to her. It wasn't about college or work. It was about doing something exciting and fun with her. But she wasn't interested, so fuck it. I'm working all the time now, and I hardly see her. And then when we are together, she's either angry or tragic. I don't look forward to seeing her, so I don't make the effort. It's not a deliberate thing, that's just the way it's worked out. It's pretty

CHRIS BINCHY

sad." He smiled at me without conviction. "Not the basis of a healthy relationship," he said then to finish.

"Have you talked to her about this?" I asked.

"We don't talk about anything else. I can't remember the last time we had a proper conversation."

"That's tough," I said.

"Yeah. Well, anyway. We'll see. I'm sorry. It's depressing stuff, and I didn't want to drag you into it."

"That's okay."

"Will you have a drink? Counselor's fee?"

"Sure."

He looked at me, then laughed.

"Jesus, you look traumatized. Don't worry. We'll sort it out. These long-term things need more work than I'm used to, that's all."

"How long has it been exactly?"

"It's long-term for me," he said. "Anyway, who are you to talk? Have you ever made it to a second week with a girl?"

"No. It's always gone downhill after day one," I said.

"There's a lesson there."

CHAPTER FIFTEEN

F rank came into the office at eleven o'clock one morning. He laughed when he saw me with a face mask on, hair white with paint dust.

"There you are," he said. "How are you doing?"

"I'm all right," I said.

"Good trip?"

"It was great," I said.

"I'm sure it was. We'll talk another time. Is he around?"

"Out the back. On the phone, I think. Are you going to help with this?"

He laughed. "Ah, no."

"Why not?"

"Because I'm not a painter."

"Neither am I."

"I know that," he said, looking around the room. "So what are you doing here?"

"Because he's paying me. I'm not a complete fool."

"Fair enough. But I wouldn't be stuck in here sanding windows for anything."

"Aren't you lucky that you're richer than me?" I said.

"I suppose I am," he said. He was walking out and then turned. "My stag is on Saturday, if you're free. Just a few people going to a pub. Nothing major."

"Yeah," I said. "I can do that. Thanks."

"It could be all right. I don't know what the plan is. I just know where we're meeting."

"Are you looking forward to it?"

"Not enormously."

"Well, I'll be there."

He sighed.

"That doesn't help me at all," he said.

In a strip club on the Saturday night with a bunch of people I didn't know there was a girl sitting beside me. She wanted to start a conversation that would end with me handing her fifty quid, and I wasn't giving it to her. I didn't want to be there anymore, and I looked around for Frank, but there was no sign of him. In the pub before we'd come to this place, I'd talked to a couple of his friends. They were a nice crowd, friendly enough. But as the night went on and they drank more, they broke into groups. The tight organic units of their friendship made sense in a place like this, where they were afraid of themselves, afraid of what they might do. Retreat to the group and hope you keep each other from straying too far. I was sitting near a few of them, but not close enough to talk. After a couple of minutes the girl left. I drank from a bottle, hoping that it might help me handle this better. Around me there were other men on their own, guys who looked turned on and depressed by girls who just seemed distracted. I wanted to go, but I couldn't leave without saying good-bye to Frank, and I couldn't wander around looking for him. Not in a place like this. So I stayed where I was. Another girl sat beside me. She was beautiful. They all were. She smiled at me, and I smiled back.

"You look lost," she said.

"I'm all right."

"Do you not like it here?" she said. Her accent came from somewhere warm, and it made me relax a bit.

"I'm just here for a friend. It's a stag thing."

"Okay. Well, you can just look. It's not so bad. You can have a drink and watch the show."

"You're right," I said. "It's not so bad." I felt a wave of love for her. She was looking after me. "Where are you from?" I asked then.

"From Martinique. In the Caribbean."

"Is that French?" I said.

"It was. Now it's an overseas territory. French people can come and live there if they want."

"I saw a film set somewhere there. Like an island paradise kind of place, right?"

"Not paradise, no. Maybe before, but now, you know, the tourism is everywhere so the culture is changing. The people are losing their identity. They have money but nothing else. So I don't know, is that better?"

"Maybe not. It's a problem," I said.

"It is," she said. "Anyway. Do you want to come into the back with me?" She stood and waited, smiling, her hand reaching out to me. "I'll dance for you and spread my ass in your face, would you like that? Really turn you on. There are things I will do that you'll never have seen. Come with me. I'll show you." She held a hand out to me.

"Thank you very much, but I won't," I said. "I'll just hang on for my friend. But thank you." She shrugged and walked off. "Nice talking to you," I said to her back as she went and I watched.

When Frank emerged from wherever he'd been, we moved on. It was almost three o'clock. He was holding it together better than his friends and wanted to go somewhere else. We had lost some people already, and a few of the others trailed off when they realized that the night wasn't over yet. Then there were four of us left, and I felt I had to stay. I was taking it easy, so I didn't mind. I could do it for Frank. We went to a place that served until five. One of them had been before, and he led us in. A sticky steamy place that got hotter as we kept going up stairs, past floors full of people. The ceilings got lower as we got higher, the music got louder, and the people got drunker. We reached the top, where there was a bar and a DJ, and Frank went to order shots of something for everybody. People were wedged into the space, holding each other up. Water dripped off the ceiling. The atmosphere was wild, messy, and loose, and it felt like if one person stepped out of line, in a moment it would turn into a riot. Frank brought the drinks over, and we knocked them back in one together. Somebody went off to get another, and I began to worry. I was talking to one of Frank's friends when across the room I saw Alex. He was leaning against the wall, talking to a girl. It was a relief. I could talk to him and stop having to try with these nice people that I didn't know. I was just tired. I excused myself and made my way over to him. He didn't see me until I was nearly in front of him. For a moment he looked like he didn't know me, as if he was struggling to recognize me out of context. He said something to the girl and took a step toward me.

"What are you doing here?" he said.

"On a stag. Guy from work. And you?"

"It's late, and it's got a bar. Where else would I be? I'm always in places like this."

"Who are you with?"

He pointed toward a group of people.

"This lot. They're doing that play I was at during the week. I met a couple of them on a set."

"Right."

The girl was standing behind him, half-smiling at me. Alex turned around.

"Hi," he said to her.

"Hi."

"I was just saying how brilliant you were. This is David. David, this is Rebecca." We shook hands. "Rebecca has a part in this play I was telling you about," he said then.

"A small part," she said.

"It was great, though. You were great."

"He's telling me this all night," she said, and I smiled. "How come I haven't met you before?" she asked me then. I didn't know what to say.

"David was away for a while. He was off in Brazil."

"That was you. I remember now. Alex told me. How was that?"

"It was great." I didn't know what was going on.

"Can you do me a favor?" Alex said to her. "Could you go to the bar for me? Get me the same again. Will you have one?"

"I'm fine," I said.

"Do you mind?"

"No," she said, "it's no problem." She leaned in to him and kissed him on the neck. She drew her hand across his stomach as she went off to the bar, a trail of intimacy in her wake.

"So that's Rebecca," he said.

"Okay," I said. He was watching her in the mirror behind the bar. "And what's the story with her?"

He shrugged.

"No story. Just a friend."

I laughed to myself.

"I'm a friend," I said. "I don't kiss you on the neck."

"You could if you wanted."

"I don't think so. Not like that." I knew he was waiting for me to ask him something more so he could spill it out. He wanted to tell me. But I just looked at him and didn't say anything else.

"Nothing's going on," he said after a minute. "I met her doing an ad a while ago and just got talking to her. She's fun. She asked me along to this thing tonight. That's all." He didn't sound convinced.

"That's all?"

"Yeah."

"Not my business, I suppose," I said.

"No. That's not what I'm saying. Just nothing's happening."

"Right."

We stood there, looking at each other. I was drunk and only realized a second before he spoke that he was raging.

"For fuck's sake," he said. "You have no idea what's been going on. You can't just turn up out of nowhere and judge me with that stupid expression on your face."

He was pulling me into it. Even if I left now, it was too late.

"What's the problem?" I said. "Decide if you're going to break up with Camille. Once you do that, you're free to do whatever you want. One thing finishes, another starts. It's your life."

"I'm not even contemplating that. There's no point in talking to you about this anymore."

"Probably not," I said.

In the mirror I watched Rebecca at the bar, talking with her friends. There was an exuberance about them, talking their way from one big laugh to the next. It was the end of their night, and things had obviously gone well. You could see their relief in every movement. They were happy.

"But if you see Camille, can you not tell her about this? If you're talking to her."

"Jesus, Alex."

"What?"

"What are you doing? I'm not your conscience, you can do what you want. But don't make me lie for you. Don't make me promise to do something like that."

"I'm not asking you to lie. I'm not asking you to do anything. I'm asking you to do nothing. That's not the same. It doesn't have to be a big issue. None of my other friends would be bothered. You wouldn't have been bothered before now."

"Maybe not," I said. "But this is different. Camille is a friend. We hang around together. Remember? The three of us?"

"Of course I remember."

"So I don't want to be scheming against her."

"That's not what it is," he said. "All I'm asking is that you don't say anything to her about this. I'll sort it out myself. But it's a complicated situation."

"I never understand why you say that. Every time, it's complicated—but I don't think it is."

"What are you talking about?"

"I've been around for the last hundred girls, don't forget, and it's always the same. The fuzzy little overlap phase where nothing's really clear and nobody knows what's going on. By the time it's all resolved, you're on to the next one. So don't pretend that you're not completely certain about what's happening. Because you always know. It's not complicated at all."

"What is wrong with you?" he said.

"I'm pissed off."

"It's not your business. You're making a big deal out of nothing."

"That's not true. Do you remember—" I stopped. Despite how wound up I was getting, I hesitated before saying more. "When you and Camille started going out, you told me that this was different. You said you'd never met a girl like her, you talked about connections and love, and I believed you. I had to believe you because otherwise I wouldn't have been able to forget about what you did."

"And what did I do exactly? Something that you would never have done. That's all. You can tell yourself that you were on the verge of grabbing her and making some passionate declaration of love, but if we're going to be honest with each other, then you'll know that I'm right. It wasn't going to happen. You can blame me for how things ended up if you want, but that won't change anything. And whatever you may think you know, I can tell you that you've no idea what it's like between us when you're not around. Are you suggesting that I should stay with her forever because you feel I owe you one?"

"No, that's not what it's about."

"Then what the fuck is it about?"

"If she was just another girl to you, I don't know why you bothered. You could have left it. Why didn't you?"

"Because there was no point. You could relive that evening fifty times, and still you'd never make a move. That's not my fault. It's just the reality of the situation." I looked at him. His face was the same, he was still the same person, even if what he said made him seem different. There was truth there, but stating it meant that the possibility that we would ever get back to normal was threatened. He obviously felt that too. "What happened here?" he said. "This was a lot easier before she was around. We never argued then. Never. I've known you for twenty years, and as soon as she arrived on the scene, the whole thing started to fall apart. Are we really going to fight over a girl? It's just stupid. Can we not go back to how we were before?"

"How happy was I then?" I asked.

He looked at me, thrown for a second.

"I don't know. You seemed all right to me."

"No. I was never all right. Hanging around in your shadow all the time."

"That's bollocks. It wasn't like that."

"It felt that way to me."

"So this is better now, is it?" he said then.

"Not really," I said. "But we can't go back."

"No, I don't think we can."

We stood there looking at each other for a second, and then I just walked away.

CHAPTER SIXTEEN

I was woken by a text from Frank at twelve the next day to see if I wanted to go for lunch. We wouldn't normally meet at the weekend, but his girlfriend was in England for the weekend. I was feeling miserable, hungover, and sore and wanted to get out of the house. We met at a place he suggested, somewhere new and wholesome. He was sitting outside wearing sunglasses and drinking coffee when I arrived.

"How are you feeling?" he asked when I sat down.

"Not too bad. You?"

He shook his head.

"Wretched. How bad was I?"

"You seemed fine."

"Really?"

"Yeah. Better than the rest of them."

"I don't remember much. I keep getting flashes, and I don't know what's real and what my imagination is filling in to punish me. Some of the things I've seen in my head make me want to go and bury myself."

"It's just the hangover. There was no drama. Nothing happened."

"Thank you for saying that. Let's eat something."

We looked at a menu, and I went in and ordered. I watched Frank through the window as he sat slumped in his chair outside, out of place among all the washed couples and shiny young families. A little puddle of darkness.

"Were you in the last place? The one with all the stairs?" he asked when I came back out.

"I was, yeah. You bought a round of shots when we arrived."

"I remember that," he said. "And you were there. When did you go?"

"Not long after. I didn't say good-bye to you."

"I wouldn't have noticed." He was turning in on himself. "I don't know how I got home. I don't know when. Who knows what I did in between? I never drink like that. I could have done anything."

"But you probably didn't."

"How did I get back?"

"I would guess you just went outside and got a taxi home. Where else would you have gone?"

"Back to the lap-dancing place?" I looked at him, trying to give him the space to keep talking if there was something there, but it was nothing.

"No," I said. "You woke up at home. You don't remember being anywhere else, so you weren't. That's it. I'd say some sort of homing instinct kicked in."

He seemed to brighten.

"Yeah," he said. "Like a pigeon. You're probably right." The food arrived, and we ate. Pancakes and bacon and juice and more coffee.

"I feel better after this conversation," he said afterward. "Exorcised a few demons. Do you get this way after drinking? This fucking endless guilt?"

"Not really."

"You're younger. It'll come in time. You look crap, if you don't mind me saying."

"I didn't sleep well."

"Why was that?"

"Do you want me to tell you? It's all about personal stuff and arguments and shit like that." I would have been happy to talk to anyone, just to get it out.

"Maybe not," Frank said. "I don't think I'm up to it. Sorry."

"That's okay."

When we were going, he asked if I wanted to do something for the afternoon. Go to a film or something. I think he was afraid of being on his own. I told him that I needed to sleep, and I left him.

Camille rang when I was on my way home. I looked at the phone buzzing in my hand, thought about letting the call go to message, but then answered.

"Were you asleep?" she asked.

"No, I'm up. It is two o'clock."

"Yeah, I suppose. Okay. Good. How are things?"

"Fine. How are you?"

"I'm all right. Look, I'm sorry to be ringing you, but you don't know where Alex is, do you?"

"No, I don't. He's not at home?"

"No."

"Working, maybe?"

"He's not supposed to be. But I can't get him. His mobile is off."

"Maybe he got called in."

"I don't know. Maybe."

"Are you all right?" I asked.

"Not really," she said. "We said earlier in the week that we'd meet on Friday, and then he never called. I left him messages, and he hasn't got back to me. I don't know what's going on."

"Are you in town?" I asked.

"I am, yeah."

"I'll meet you."

"What for?"

"It's just easier than talking on the phone. Are you free?"

"Yes, I suppose I am."

Fifteen minutes later I met her outside a café. She was warm when she arrived, hugging me close and smiling, but I could see she wasn't all right. We talked about nothing for a while, and then she asked about Alex again.

"You're not worried about him, are you? You don't think something's wrong."

I didn't know when I arranged to meet her that I was going to tell her everything, but with her there beside me I had no option. Fuck him. Why should I lie? Why should I let her suffer?

"He's fine," I said. "There's nothing wrong with him."

"How do you know?"

"I saw him last night."

"Where?"

"In some late-night shithole in town."

"When was this?"

"At about three in the morning."

"Was he all right? He's not sick or having a breakdown or anything?"

"He's fine. Nothing like that."

She processed this for a moment.

"What was he doing? Who was he with?"

"I don't know what he was doing. Drinking, I think. And he was with some crowd of actors or a theater group or something. People he knows through work."

She shook her head and looked off in the other direction.

"What is he doing? I know he's your friend and everything, and I don't want to make you uncomfortable, but why is he being such a shit? If he wants to go out with friends, that's fine, but why wouldn't he let me know what's happening? Answer the phone or return my messages? Does he think I've nothing better to be doing than hanging around waiting for him to get in touch? Has he just given up?"

"I don't know," I said. "I don't know what he's at. He's being an idiot."

"Were you talking to him?"

"I was, yeah."

"And what was he saying?"

"Nothing. He didn't mention you. Just said he was out with this crowd who had finished doing a play."

"That's all."

I shrugged.

"Pretty much." I nearly spoke, then stopped. It was harder than I'd expected.

"What?" she said. "Go on, David. Tell me."

"I'm only saying this because . . ." I couldn't think of anything else to say.

"What?" she said again.

"No, just he was there with some girl, you know? I don't understand what he's doing."

"With a girl?" she said. "What do you mean 'with a girl'?"

"Nothing. Just that. He was there, and there was a girl with him."

"Who was she?"

"I don't know."

"So was she just one of the crowd?"

"Camille . . . ," I said.

"What? What? Just tell me what you mean. I have no idea what to think. Why are you telling me he was with a girl? Do you think he's sleeping with her? Is that it?"

"I don't know. Maybe," I said.

"Really," she said, and then went quiet.

I breathed in deep.

"Listen, I met him and he was with this girl and they looked pretty close. I asked him what was going on, and he said it was nothing, and I'm only telling you because I think he's being an arsehole and that you should know."

"Okay," she said.

"He's not a reliable person," I said. "He's great and he's fun and he can be very kind and generous and everything. He's my oldest friend, and I love him. But things don't last with him. He just loses interest or loses his way or whatever. I don't know why. I've seen this kind of thing twenty times before. But I thought it would be different with you."

"I don't know anything about that. I never thought he'd cheat on me. Never," she said.

"I'm not saying that he did. I'm just letting you know what I saw because I care for you, and I think it's wrong of him to treat you like this."

"But you think he's up to something? You think he's fucking somebody else?" She was staring at me now, and I could see she was close to crying. There was nowhere for me to go.

"Yes, I do," I said and I held her gaze.

"Thank you," she said. "Thanks for telling me."

"I'm on your side," I said. I reached over and held her hand. She didn't pull away, but it felt like the wrong thing to have done. She looked at me, smiled a very unhappy smile, then stood up.

"I'll go on," she said.

"Where are you going?"

"I'll call over to his flat and see if he's there."

"Okay." I stood. "Do you want me to come with you?"

"No. I don't think so."

"All right." I hugged her. "You're so lovely," I said into her hair. "I'm sorry to have to tell you all this. He's just such a fucking idiot."

"Thanks," she said, and then she was gone.

Everything I had told her was true. It had to be done. When

I realized the night before that for Alex this was just the latest complicated disengagement he would have to endure, my loyalty switched, and once that happened, I had to let her know. She would go to his house now, and if the Rebecca girl was there, Camille might not even need to talk to him. She could just walk away, and that would be the end of it. She would be free of it all. It was beginning to diminish her. I'd seen that since coming back. It was there in her voice and the way she carried herself. Not beaten yet but fading.

But I could admit that I wanted him to be caught as well. I wanted her to see what he was doing and for him to have to respond. Let him tell her that it was complicated. Let him know that I was on her side and that he was on his own, because what he did was wrong. Let that idea sink into his head and wake him up to what was going on.

I walked home though the Saturday-afternoon shoppers in town. At some point, I thought, my phone would ring again that day. She would call to tell me what had happened, or he would ring, outraged and demanding to know why I had betrayed him. I was ready for either scenario. Camille would be arriving at his place in the next ten minutes. I could picture it. I knew the sound that the buzzer would make and the crackle when somebody picked up inside. I wondered if she would give up if there was no response and hoped that she would stand there and ring again and again until before he knew what he was doing he would buzz her in. I waited for the pulse of the phone in my hand to tell me that something had happened, but that afternoon it never came.

CHAPTER SEVENTEEN

The doorbell rang at close to midnight. I was at home, dozing in front of the television. Alex, I thought, this is going to be a fight. But when I went to the intercom it was Camille. I buzzed her in and waited at the door until she came into the landing.

"Is it too late?" she said.

"For what?"

"You're still up, I mean."

"I am, yeah. Come in."

She sat on the couch, and I opened a bottle of wine.

"So?" I said as I sat beside her. "Did you see him?"

"Oh, yeah."

"And was it all right?"

"No. Not really. Have you talked to him?"

"No. Why?"

She laughed.

"You'll be hearing from him, I think. He's definitely not happy with you."

I could see now that she'd been out. She didn't seem drunk, but she was flushed and buzzy and the air around her seemed to crackle.

"That's fair enough. I'll deal with that when I have to. How did you get on?"

"It's just not going to work, is it?"

"I don't know," I said. "What do you mean?"

"Well, this is the way he does things, right? You said that. You've seen this before."

"What happened?"

"So after I left you, I found him and asked about where he'd been and he said he'd been out with friends and that he was sorry for not having got in touch. So I told him what you'd said and asked him who the girl was and he said she was nobody. I asked again, and he said that she's a friend but that he likes her, and somewhere around there it just blew up. He was saying he's got too much going on and feels like he's under a lot of pressure and that maybe a relationship isn't the thing for him right now, and I told him to fuck himself basically, that if he wants to do other things and do other people then he should have the balls to just say so, not stop answering his phone or responding to messages or talk about commitments and pressure. I'm not going to chase a boyfriend around or wait for him to call or try and coax him into seeing me. I don't need to do that. I'm not going to be the pathetic girl at home who doesn't know what's going on while he's out meeting girls who are friends that he likes. So I told him to say whether he wanted to try and keep this going or not, and he said he didn't know. So I think that's probably it."

"Okay," I said. "I'm sorry."

"It's fine. Seriously. I went out and met Fiona, and actually I feel all right. I was on my way home but then I thought I'd see if you were up so I could tell you what the story was. And I wanted to thank you. I didn't really say that to you earlier, but I know that it's a big thing for you to look out for me when he's been your friend for so long."

"I just didn't like it."

"You're a good friend," she said and held my hand, then rested her head on my shoulder. We sat in silence. She wasn't crying, but she was very still, and I thought at any stage she might start. There was nobody else around, and the house was quiet. I could have sat there all night but then she spoke.

"I have to leave," she said.

"Are you sure? You can stay if you want." I said it casually, and she didn't seem to notice.

"No, I better go," she said.

We stood and walked to the door.

"Thanks a lot," she said, and she looked up at me. I could see that she was exhausted.

"It'll get better," I said as if I knew.

"Thanks."

I kissed her cheek and held her. Then I kissed her again, quick and then slower. I knew the next time it was going to be something else, and as soon as I realized that, I hesitated.

"No," she said. "I have to go." She took a step back and I let her go, but she didn't go any farther. We stood looking at each other, waiting for the next thing to happen.

"Just stay," I said and leaned forward and kissed her deep on the mouth and then she kissed me back and I became aware that she was with me now and we were walking together toward my bedroom. There were things I could have been thinking, calculations I might have made or anxieties about why it was happening. Maybe she was drunker than I'd thought.

But in a moment like that, how much space do you allow the voices that tell you to stop? You don't want to know. We stood at the edge of the bed, holding hands, face to face, saying nothing, and we surely both knew what was going to happen next. Every idea that I tried to hold on to slipped away as soon as it was thought. Then we were on the bed and she was lying back. I lay across her and we were kissing again and the world outside with its shadows and light, with its people everywhere doing things, drifted away. They were all getting it wrong and this was where I was and all I needed to know was here. What about him? I thought. Can I do this? I stopped and pushed myself back off for a second. I saw her looking up at me for the first time. Her eyes were sleepy, but she was all right.

"What about Alex? What's he going to say?"

"What can he say?" she said, and that was it. That was all I thought about him, because we were in my bedroom, and when she began to pull at my clothes I knew that it wasn't going to stop. As I unbuttoned and unzipped her clothes, she shifted and turned and I felt her skin now. Under the covers of my bed. Breathing and warmth. Closeness. You get closer and closer, and what does that do to you? This new place that you come to, it seems like nothing, commonplace and easy when you are there, but everything tells you that it can't be as simple as this. That there must be consequences, that something has to happen next. But why? Why does it have to be anything more than what it is? It was Camille, and I knew her. She wasn't going to turn into a stranger overnight. I could see her now and feel her beneath me, smell her skin and lose a sense of what was her and what was me.

It was a dream. The strangeness of a situation that you feel you've been in before but can't quite remember, everything moving to a place that you know but can't imagine. I had thought about it before. Of course I had. Every night the shape that came to me was her. Every time I saw her I held on to as much as I could. But now with her in front of me, lying beside me, moving, I tried to catch the rhythm that she was in.

"Is this okay?" I said, checking again to be sure, because I couldn't believe that this was where we were.

"Yes," she said, quickly. "It's fine."

"It's all I ever wanted," I said into her neck at a time when I had never been closer to her.

In the morning I was aware of everything before I was fully awake. When I moved, I could tell that she was still there. I turned over and looked at the back of her head, the darkness of her hair against the pillow. The skin of her neck that I already knew, her shoulders, the top of her back. The inward curve of her body that the bedclothes followed in and then out again.

My head was thick with tiredness. I would have to talk to her and find out what was going to happen next, but I could allow myself this moment of pleasure. There was an empty space where guilt should have been. Alex had tried with her. The two of them had struggled to make it work together, and it was clear that he had already started moving on, too early, before she knew what was happening. So why should I feel guilt? Who knew where he had ended up the night before, out in the thick of it on a Friday, where everybody in a thousand places in town set out to get what they wanted, not thinking of the people at home. The others, left behind. He could keep it all. It was an ending. That was what it was. A marker made by me and her to signal the end of one stage, the beginning of another. Why should I be thoughtful, delicate, measured? I had loved her from when I met her first, and when I'd got to know her, that just intensified. Surely I was allowed in this moment, waking with everything new about her still fresh in my memory, to be unqualified in my happiness.

She was here and we were together and it felt like I should know her even better now, and yet I was too uncertain to touch her. As she began to move, I felt the questions start to rise in me. What if it was a mistake for her? A drunken impulse that would have to be faced in the next thirty seconds? Circumstances had somehow cast a spell that now would be broken by her waking. I didn't deserve her, and I knew it. Alex had been right all along. This was a fantasy for me. It was a dream. But then she woke, and she rolled over. When she saw me, I watched her in a second process the memory of where she was. In that instant of analysis I thought my heart was going to stop, but then she sort of smiled.

"Hi," I said. "You're still here."

"I was asleep," she said. She sat up. "What time is it?"

"Nearly eight."

"Okay." She thought for a second, putting shape on her day. "I've got to go," she said then. "My parents are coming over later, and I need to be there."

She got up, found her clothes on the floor beside the bed, and left the room without looking back. I got dressed and was sitting on the bed when she came back in. She sat beside me and put a hand on the back of my neck.

"You understand this, don't you?"

"I think so."

"I'll maybe ring you later on," she said.

"Sure. No problem."

She kissed me on the side of the face, and I turned. She kissed me again on the lips, but so quickly that it didn't seem to mean anything.

"Are you all right?" I asked. "This wasn't some horrible mistake, was it?"

"Listen. David," she said. When I heard my name I breathed in and held, but it didn't come. "You know the whole story with Alex. You know it's all a mess and I know we'll have to talk about it sometime but can we not do it now, just leave it for tonight? I'm not ready for it yet. Is that okay?"

"It's fine," I said.

"You're a friend, you know," she was saying. "A good friend. But I don't know what I'm going to do now. And I think it'd be better if we just don't talk to each other for a while."

"Who? Me and you?"

"Just until I sort out what's going on in my head. Would that be all right?" I didn't say anything. Just looked at her. Her hand was still on mine. She pulsed it, a little flex, smiled crooked at me. "Nothing to say?"

"It's not what I wanted to hear," I said.

"You understand, though. Don't you? I'm not going to do something now and then in a week or two discover it was the wrong thing to have done. Hurt us both more. And you. You can see that I have to wait until I know what I want to happen."

"I do," I said. "It's just that I don't have any of your doubts. I've known since I met you. Since then."

"Really?"

"You didn't know?"

"No."

"Well, there you go." We looked at each other. There was nothing in her expression that told me anything. She just looked at me, blankly, as if she hadn't understood what I'd said to her.

"You could have said something," she said then.

"Not really. The right moment never arrived." I smiled at her. "Is this bad timing?"

"I'm all over the place," she said. "I need to get my head together. That's all. I'll call you in a week."

"A week?"

"No longer than that. Is that okay?"

"Yeah. Okay. Yeah."

"You look pretty desolate." She was almost smiling at me.

"I love you," I said out of nowhere.

"I'll ring you," she said and kissed me, too quick and light, then went to go. She stopped after a second. "Thanks again," she said as she went.

I understood what she had said to me. I could see her point about needing to let things settle before making a decision about what she wanted to do and all that. I could do a good job of appearing reasonable, but I hated it, and even before she was out of the building I knew that the whole week would be taken up with me blaming myself for not having done it differently.

Because in that time anything could happen. Whatever good there might have been in it could be turned inside out as she thought it through. Maybe it had been the right thing to do—declaring my love like a panicking informer ratting out of habit. Maybe it would make her see me differently. But already I was realizing that there were situations that were just beyond my capabilities and that I was out of my depth. I thought I could read people, that years of standing back and watching gave me some special insight, but it gave me nothing. Seeing what people do tells you nothing about why they're doing it. It tells you nothing about what they'll do next. Even with Alex and Camille, people that I knew so well, I couldn't say what would happen.

I would be assessed. But when I tried to look at it from her perspective, I saw that there never had been three people involved, it was just the two of them. When in the end a third person came along, destabilizing the situation, it wasn't me—it was that Rebecca girl. For Camille, I was a friend giving comfort when she was down. That was all.

It made sense, the two of us together. We knew each other. We knew we liked each other. The strangeness of sleeping with her was only that it hadn't happened before. She needed me, and I was there. I made no pretense to myself that day that I would do anything else. I just sat in front of the TV with the phone beside me, waiting to hear from someone. I drank black coffee because the milk had gone off, clumping down the sink. In the afternoon I watched horses racing, a biblical epic, a dance competition. It would make you want to give up. I ordered a pizza, and then when the doorbell rang, I let myself hope that it might be her. I slept on the couch and in the morning moved into the bedroom. Was this what I was going to do for the week? Just sit back and wait until something happened? A week could even be a loose term. How specific did I expect her to be? When was it all right for me to ring her? And how would I start that conversation? Just wondering what you'd decided . . . Any news? Yes or no? Me or him?

I wouldn't be capable of that, and so I would have to wait. Because no matter what way I looked at it, I knew that if she had something to tell me, she would, but every hour that passed, the outcome seemed more and more inevitable. I went to work on the Monday morning, underslept, with a gloom that O'Toole bollocked out of me in five minutes. He was all fired up and enthusiastic, and I saw that the freshness of it was a space to live in. The nervy drudgery of starting something new would hold me. We were setting it up as an office, carrying things in from vans, moving furniture around, and making calls to suppliers. I got home late every evening and just ate and went to bed. I could stop myself from thinking about her. There was enough going on. I shut it down when the questions came to me and thought of something else. Targets. Deadlines. Drinks at the weekend. Happy little exchanges with people at work. Phone conversations. Saying hello and thank you to people in shops. That was where I was. I could compartmentalize. There was a part of my mind that would stay shut down, while I contemplated the possibilities of work. But by Thursday I was numb, trying to ignore it.

CHAPTER EIGHTEEN

Alex called on the Friday after work and said that he wanted to meet. I asked him when, and he said as soon as possible and named a place. There was no chat, not a word beyond what was necessary. He wasn't there when I arrived, so I ordered a drink and sat at a table near the door, away from the work people standing at the bar in a shouting, staggering group. He nodded when he saw me, walked over, and sat down. He didn't get a drink.

"How are you?" I asked. He said nothing in response. Just sat looking at me with no particular expression on his face. "Are you all right? What's going on?"

"Do you have anything to tell me?" he said.

"I don't think so. I assume you know everything."

"No, I don't."

I didn't know what to say. I had known at all stages that this conversation was coming, but still I wasn't ready.

"What are you talking about?" I said.

"I don't know how you could do the things you've done. I don't understand why you would be such a fucking disloyal bastard, why you would want to hurt me like this. I have never in my life said a bad word about you. Not once. We've been friends for twenty years. What happened to you? Why did you suddenly turn against me?"

"I didn't. I'm not against you."

"Telling her lies about me. What did you think you saw in that nightclub? You met me talking to a girl, and you immediately assumed I was cheating on Camille, based on nothing."

"No, that wasn't it at all."

"Well, what was it? Because after I talked to you, all drunk and full of irrational outrage spoiling for a fight, the next day Camille comes over and practically kicks my door in, telling me that she knows I'm having an affair. Where did this come from, I wondered to myself, never even considering the prospect that you'd have been so nasty as to tell outright lies about me. But then she tells me that you saw me with someone and that you thought it looked as if I was sleeping with this girl. Which is a bit of a fucking stretch considering that, first, I hadn't done anything to make you think that, and secondly, I told you I wasn't. You asked me what was going on, and I told you—nothing. Because nothing was. So why did you tell Camille that you had your doubts or suspicions or whatever it was? Why was that, David?"

"Because I did. You said that girl was a friend or whatever, and I just didn't believe you. That's all."

"Why would I lie? Am I not honest with you? Have I not told you the truth since I've known you?"

"Yes, I think so."

"Then why wouldn't you believe me?"

"Because I just don't trust you anymore." I didn't even know what I was saying. The words were coming out of me somehow, and all I could do was listen to them. They sounded forthright, certain, defiant.

"Why?" he asked.

"I don't know," I said. "The whole Camille thing."

"Oh, for fuck's sake," he said. "You told me that was resolved."

"I thought it was. But obviously it's not."

"There's nothing I can do about that now. It makes no difference anyway. You don't have the right to lie about me, to freak Camille out for no good reason, to try and fuck things up for me out of some sense of entitlement or revenge or whatever it was."

"I know what I saw," I said.

"What? What did you see?"

"You out with some young one at three in the morning, while your girlfriend's ringing your phone and leaving messages with no idea where you are. I saw how that girl kissed you and how turned on you were by the fact that you had to pretend it was nothing because I was there. I saw you back in your element with one girl desperate and heartbroken trying to keep up with you, and another throwing herself at you, all easy and fun but off the record for the moment. None of this is new. You do the same thing every time, use the same words, the same serious facial expression and tone of voice."

"Bollocks," he said. "You tried to fuck this up because of Camille. Out of jealousy and meanness. Because I had something that you wanted but couldn't have. If you think that's what you saw the other night and you think that's why you did what you did, then you're deluding yourself. I told you that Camille and I were having a bad time and that it was a struggle. But I didn't say I was giving up. I didn't tell you that I wanted to end it. I fucking told you that we would sort it out, and still on the basis of nothing you went to her, planting doubts in her head."

"She came to me."

"It makes no difference. I would have thought that you'd tell her the truth. That's all. Nothing more. But then if you don't trust me, why would you bother?"

"I'm sorry," I said. "I didn't mean that. It just came out."

We sat in silence for a moment. Around us the Friday-night crowd was drinking and laughing, oblivious to our conversation.

"But can I trust you?" he said. "Do you want to talk about that?" I looked at him.

"What do you mean?"

"Did you think I wouldn't know? That she wouldn't tell me? What were you thinking?"

"I don't know," I said.

"You must know. Of course you fucking know. All the shit you gave me. Were you trying to pay me back?"

"No. Not at all. Not for a second."

"Then what?"

"I don't know. It just happened."

"What happened?"

I couldn't speak. There was nothing I could think of to say.

"What happened, David? Go on. I've heard it already from her, but why don't you tell me. Being so honest and all."

"Nothing," I said.

"Nothing? That's not what she said at all."

"Just fucking leave it, Alex, will you? I'm sorry. I thought it was over between you."

He laughed, a cold little bark.

"Now who's lying? I have to go, but I'll tell you two things first. Even if it was over, even if she had a sworn declaration saying it was true, I would have expected you to stay the fuck away for a year or two out of respect. For me or for us or for our friendship. I wouldn't ever have questioned that.

"And secondly, we are going to try and sort this out, Camille and I, despite you and your fucking around, but while we do that, maybe you could leave us alone. Is that okay?"

I said nothing. I could feel a buzzing in my head, gray dots that cleared as soon as they came.

"Right," I said. I looked at him and saw his face and recognized something about it, but the person I knew was gone. He stared back at me, then stood up.

"Hang on. Alex—"

"That's it," he said. "That's all."

He left, knocking off the table as he went. A pint glass wobbled, then spilled and rolled onto the floor as he left. The bar went quiet with the crash, and the crowd turned and looked at me sitting alone. A few of them cheered, all ironic and drunk, and then in a moment the noise was back to what it had been before.

It wasn't guilt at first. It wasn't regret or loss or anger. It was embarrassment. The sheer humiliation of it. Of knowing that she had been with him and with me, and in the end, she still went for him. The realization now that I had been a mistake, a moment of stupidity and regret. That maybe she had seen me as a route back to him. The idea was there formed and ready to be thought. That it was a cry to him for attention. Look what I will do without you, she was saying. See what I can do. She would say that she had been confused and I had been there and I had made the first move on her. Because that was true. Wasn't it? It couldn't have been her idea. I tried to remember the moment and felt already how the memory had turned, corrupted now by doubt. I could identify the point at which everything began to collapse. I did it myself. It was my fault.

To know the things that he could tell her now. The whole story from the beginning—the life I'd imagined with her and how I'd frozen him out when the two of them got together. The jealousy and bitterness. The forgiveness. The way I'd hung around on the edges of their relationship, waiting for something to happen. Watching in case he slipped up, judging him when he did, and moving in on her. Presenting myself as the loyal friend who could see it all from her point of view, telling her that the problem wasn't with her, it was him. It was him and his philandering, his bad temper, his indecision, his reluctance to commit to her. The implications of everything

I'd ever said to her. Alex is a nice fellow. He's a good guy, he's fun, you know? But you should realize that he will not do the things you expect. He has his demons. His inconsistencies. His failings that we will not talk about but which we know are there. In the space between the bad and the good news, with the moment of hesitation when asked to vouch for his intentions, I had given her some bland blasé platitude. I planted doubt. I'm sure he'd tell you if there was something wrong. Of course he wants you to go to New York with him. Of course. He won't go if you don't. Probably.

Was that what I'd said? Was that the impression I had left with her, undermining him all the time, qualifying my comments about him in a way that left enough space for uncertainty to get in and spread like rot? Had I done all this? I told myself at the time that I was being balanced, that I couldn't say what I didn't know. But of course I could. That's what I should have been doing. It was what he would presume. Yes. Absolutely. Great guy. He'll be good to you. He loves you. He cares. No doubt. I could have said it all and made it real for her. It was what he would have done for me.

When he came to me to talk about his problems and doubts and worries, did I do anything more than wag my finger at him, tell him what he was doing wrong, tell him to try harder, be better, do the right thing? This easygoing front, the confidence and swagger and charm, the ease that he had with people. I knew more than anyone that it cost him. There was a role for me in his life, and I knew what it was. It was to cluck and scold and pretend to know exactly what he should be doing, but also to support him and tell him that he was all right. A moral sounding board. Somebody who knew everything about him and was still here. Because he was a good guy.

Oh, I could look at it all and take the other view. That he stole Camille from me. That he was never seriously interested in her, and that the pretense that he was ran out of steam in a couple of months. That he actively tried to drive her away by saying that he was leaving, asking her and then sulking and withdrawing when she hesitated. That mentally he was long gone by the time he met Rebecca. That when Camille was left behind, wondering what had happened, I was entitled to support her, and if something happened between us, then it was a good thing. Good for her and for me. A happy ending.

But the weakness of this version was that it didn't happen like that. She went back to him, and I was left with that knowledge in the weeks that followed. It darkened everything. I wonder what they're doing now. I wonder what he's saying to her at this moment, if by just thinking of him I've triggered an impulse in his brain.

"Here's another thing," I imagined him saying to her, "another thing about that fucker that you just won't believe. And you thought he was such a nice boy."

He could say what he wanted, and given the situation in which he found himself, he probably would.

After two weeks, when I felt I could do it, I rang him. The phone buzzed and then cut to message. I thought about sending a text, that it might be easier to express myself in words, but it felt wrong. So I said nothing and let the fact that I had called speak for itself.

He rang me back a week later.

"All right," he said. A statement. Sounding normal.

"Yeah. And you?"

"Yeah."

"Listen," I said. "I'm sorry. Really."

"It's done now. There's no point worrying about it."

"But I have to tell you. It was wrong of me."

"I don't care," he said, too quick and too loud. I waited. "I rang you because I'm going off tomorrow, and I thought I should talk to you before I went."

"Going where?"

"Paris."

"Really. What, for a while like?"

"Don't know. The year, I suppose. I'm not going back to college. Maybe next year."

"What happened to New York?"

"Oh, money. Visas. All that. Too much hassle, so we're doing this instead."

"Okay."

"So anyway, I thought I'd let you know."

"Do you want to meet up for a drink or something? It would be good to see you before you go." There was a pause, the noise of a bus passing on the street wherever he was.

"Not really," he said. "I've just got a lot of stuff to get organized."

"Okay. Well, again, I'm sorry."

"Yeah. It didn't matter anyway. I'll give you a ring maybe at Christmas."

I didn't know half of what he meant. I had to say it. It was stupid to pretend to myself that I wouldn't.

"Is Camille going with you?"

He laughed. It was a laugh I knew so well that I remembered for a second how close he should be. His voice was wrong when he spoke.

"No. That didn't work out. There was nothing there really. Just delaying the inevitable."

"I'm sorry to hear it."

"Don't be," he said. He waited. "It's a fucking mess, isn't it? After all this time."

"Yes," I said. "But I'll see you when you come back. I'll talk to you then, and we'll sort it out maybe."

"Yeah. Well, anyway. Good luck or whatever."

"And you." I waited for a second and then realized that he was already gone.

She had used me to make him jealous. She went back to him, and she told him everything. She wrecked the friendship that he and I had to force him into doing something. She had come between us. The night that I saw her first, I could have turned away. Normally I would have, but I did what I did, and this was where it brought us. Having rejected me, she had ended up being rejected herself. This inclination, the urge to see everything balance out, the sense that there is order in the universe—what comfort could it give me? As soon as I thought it, it faded into nothing. It wasn't real. It didn't bring me any closer to what I wanted.

There were other things in my life. A job I could commit to. A bigger world and a life beyond what I had experienced. It could be the start of something for me. At Christmas I would see him, and we would sort it all out when the blood had cooled. In the moments after I spoke to him, I began to realize what it would be like without him. There was nobody I could call to talk about it all, just to tell them what had happened. I thought of my parents. Of Frank. Of Camille. I got up off the couch at home and left, thinking it would be easier to get out of the flat. Out on the street with people around me doing things like normal people did. Not moping around a flat on their own thinking about loneliness and isolation. I walked into town, not really knowing where I was going. It was eight o'clock. Dark on a cold October evening, the sky purple and clean and still. It was an evening for doing nothing. For waiting. The people walking toward me seemed to pick up on it, going home with shopping bags and bottles. Clinking. Talking on the phone to people they wouldn't see that night. Conversations with their mothers. People at home in the country. Friends who they'd see the next day because the next day was a Friday and that's what they were for. But not tonight. How many people in my area pulled back into their own space in the evenings? Closed the curtains. Made a meal. Ate it on their own and then later went to bed. Over and over until there was somebody else.

There were others. Tennis club types. People who did things. Not me ever. I knew who I was, and I could do it. Retreat. Lock the door. Go to work tomorrow, and afterward I would go to the pub with whomever was there and I would be glad of them. I would talk and get to know them and we would build it into something more than it was now. Work colleagues. These were people I could do things with. Look up some of the old college crowd. Reunion. See what they were at, tell them about me. Fuck it. No to it all. I wanted none of it.

CHAPTER NINETEEN

I rang her to find out. To tell her what I thought. To try and find a way of asking why she didn't see things the same way as me. I rang her because I had to. I waited as long as I could, but in the end it was only a couple of days. She was still there, and it wasn't finished.

"Hi," she said when she heard me. No surprise.

"Hello. Are you all right?"

"I'm okay. How are you?"

"Not bad."

"I've been meaning to ring you. I just haven't with everything going on. Did you talk to Alex?"

"Yeah."

"So you know the story."

"More or less. He's going."

"Yeah. Well. He's gone."

"I was sorry to hear it didn't work out," I said.

"Thanks."

"And you're all right?"

"I'm fine. Or I will be. How's work?"

"It's grand."

We were stuck. I was about to ask her how everything was again when she asked if I wanted to meet her.

I went to a pub near her flat full of rich young fellows thinking they were slumming it among the unhappy gravelly mumblers at the bar. I sat at a table away from them all and ordered from the Chinese girl who came around. When Camille arrived, I heard the noise drop and watched her walk through the bar, saw the men turning after her.

"So," she said. "Here you are." She was trying to be normal.

"You look well," I said. I stood and kissed the side of her face. She laughed.

"Me? Thanks."

"What?"

"I've not been having the best week of my life."

"Right," I said two seconds too late. Punishing her for something.

She sat beside me, and neither of us said anything for a moment. The silence threatened to grow. We sat looking across the room through the open door onto the street outside. Everything was out there. There was nothing here between us, sitting beside each other but not able to look, not able to say anything. The bridge between us was gone now. It was Alex that had linked us together, and to have even thought anything else seemed stupid. I was ready to stand up and leave when she spoke.

"I'm sorry for not ringing you before now," she said. "I wanted to explain to you what had happened."

"I know what happened. Alex told me."

"I should have rung you. I said I would."

"Yeah, but don't worry about it. It's not as if I was waiting." I tried to smile to make it seem like a joke, but got it wrong. She looked away.

"What did he say to you?" she asked when she turned back.

I shook my head.

"There's not much point in that. Is there?"

"What?"

"Going down that road. Because I don't remember exactly what he said. He told me that you had gone back to him, and the second time I spoke to him, he said it didn't work out and that he was going to France." She waited.

"That was it?" she asked then.

"Pretty much. Yeah."

"That's all he said to you before he went?"

"Just about. Well, no, there was the whole conversation about you as well. But I'm sure you know how that went."

"I don't."

"You can guess."

"No," she said. "I can't."

"He thought I'd turned against him, betrayed him, let him down. That it was unforgivable for me to get involved with you, and that I'd deliberately tried to break the two of you up out of bitterness and jealousy. He told me that he would never have done the same thing if the situation was reversed. That sort of thing." She was staring at me now. "He didn't tell you this?"

"He said nothing to me about you. Nothing at all."

"That's fair enough, I suppose."

"And was he right, do you think?"

"About that? I don't know. I denied it all, but I can't remember what I was thinking or why I did what I did. It doesn't matter now. That's all over." I remembered how it had been only a few weeks before, how it would have been, the three of us out together, and how different I would have felt then. I could say what I wanted to her now, but what good was it to me? "Why did you go back to him?" I said then. "I couldn't understand it when he told me. And why did you tell him about us? What possible purpose did that serve? He's gone, and it's you and me looking at each other in a pub, and none of us is happy now. We all have to move on." She didn't answer, just stared ahead. "I'm not blaming you for anything," I said. "But I just don't understand it."

"I love him," she said, as if that made everything fit.

"I know. But so what? Really, what difference does that make?"

"I thought we could get back to where we started from. I'm not sure it was ever possible, but I tried, and he did too. Or to prove to me that he was serious."

"But why did you tell him?"

"What?"

"About us. If you were going to go back to him and try and work it out, why did you come to my flat that night?"

"I wasn't thinking that way. I hadn't worked it out. I didn't know what I was going to do. I was all over the place. Come on. You can't put it all on me. You were there too. It just happened."

"I know. But I thought it was what you wanted."

"Really?" She looked at me now. "That's what was going on? You were helping me out."

"I don't know. I just can't understand why you had to tell him."

"I should have lied? Is that it?"

"If you wanted to get back with him, yes. You must have known that telling him was going to mess with his head. That it would hurt him and fuck everything up. It couldn't go back to the way it was after that."

"He needed to know."

"Needed?"

"Yes. Yes."

"Why?"

"I don't understand what you're saying to me. Of course I told him. He would have known. You would have told him, or I would, or something wouldn't have been right and he would have guessed. I couldn't not tell him. I wanted him to know so that he could decide if he wanted to give it another go. Knowing everything."

"Oh, who knows everything?" I said. "Nobody. It's not a right."

"That's just how I saw it. Maybe it would have been different if I hadn't, but I couldn't lie to him. You have to understand that."

"I don't," I said. "Really, I just don't."

We said nothing for a moment, trying to work out something that didn't matter. The two of us talking about him as if he was a ghost, arguing about what each of us had meant and thought and wanted even though we had barely known at the time. There were all these different versions of events, but at this stage the reality wasn't important.

Where was he now? At this precise moment what was he doing? Had he moved on? I could picture him, standing at the counter of a better bar than this with people that he had met in the afternoon. A vision of it came to me. He'd be with a mix of guys and a girl. There would be scarves and it would be cold outside. They would have drunk a bottle more than they would have intended in the afternoon and would be making a plan for later. The girl's eyes would stay a half second too long with him when he spoke to let him know what she wanted, and he would understand. He would have seen where it was all going.

Camille and I sat together, trying to work out what had happened, as if this was an equation that could be calculated from the information that we had, as if there was a solution that we could find if we talked about it for long enough. It could end anywhere. The two of us could walk out of this pub and never speak again if we let the conversation drift half a sentence too far into anger or blame. That could become the answer—a clean break at the end of it all. She might understand that without me, it would all have been different. It could have worked out for the two of them. She wouldn't be here with me now, left behind, forced into a role she didn't want to play.

"How do we get back to normal?" I asked.

"Who's 'we'? What are you talking about?"

"You and me."

"I don't know. What is normal for you and me? Alex was always around."

"Not always."

"But it was mostly the three of us." A pause to remember. A twinge. Then she spoke again. She was clear. "Were you waiting around to see what would happen between me and him? Is that why you were there all the time?"

"No," I said. "I don't know. I was just hanging around with him because I always did. And when you came along, I liked you."

"Thanks," she said.

"Maybe subconsciously," I said then. "I don't know for sure. I mean, I could ask, did you sleep with me to make him jealous?"

"No," she said. "I was just confused and pissed off, and I didn't know what I was doing."

I smiled at the floor.

"That's what every guy wants to hear from a girl he's slept with."

"I still think of you as a friend," she said.

"Okay. That's something." I nodded, and she nodded back at me. It was very tidy. It seemed likely that we both might laugh. "I still do," I said, "have a certain regard for you."

"Well, you should," she said. "I deserve it."

"So is there anything else to say?"

"Maybe not for now," she said. "But if I want to talk to you about it again, I can. Right?"

"Sure. Okay."

I thought I should maybe do something, clink her glass or

shake her hand or kiss her or some stupid thing, but in the end we just sat there looking out across the room.

"I have to meet people in town in a while," she said then. "But we must meet up again some time."

"You arranged to go out after meeting me?" I said as we stood to leave. "What did you think was going to happen here?"

"This," she said. "Exactly this."

"Really?"

"No, stupid. I had no idea," she said, and she laughed.

I worked through the autumn, the days getting shorter until I saw none of them. Dark when I left the house and dark when I got home. On Fridays I went out with Frank and the others and drank. The job wasn't what I thought it would be. The excitement and enthusiasm of the idea was hard to square with the day-to-day plodding. O'Toole was hardly ever around, off at meetings the whole time, but when he was, he cajoled and shouted and rarely encouraged. If you stood back, you could see that what we were doing was close enough to the big idea, but when you were in it, it felt like nothing. The same as before but less secure.

There was a hole in my life where Alex used to be, a space that hadn't been filled. I tried to occupy myself with work, but I knew it was there. I met Camille sometimes for lunch or out at weekends with her friends, and I knew that she was feeling the same lack. We never spoke about it, never said his name, but we hung around like people who had been through some great trauma together. It was something we would never mention, but knowing that the other person felt the same way was enough. There was nothing to be said. We were both missing him. The rights and wrongs of it didn't make any difference. He was gone, and we weren't talking about him.

But then it began to fade. We established our own space between the two of us. Meeting on weekend mornings and spending the days together. Shopping for food or wandering around looking at clothes with her, admiring everything and smiling patiently through it all because there was nowhere else I would rather be. There was nowhere else I could be. I knew that her friends must have been wondering. Whenever her phone rang and the conversation started, she would say when asked, "I'm with David," no explanation, and after a while it became so normal that it seemed there was nothing to say about it.

But there must have been. The two of us turning up together all the time. These friends must have known what had happened. What we had done together. They were friendly to me, I never felt like I was getting in the way, but it didn't feel right either. Because I had no role. I was her friend, but really I was his friend. Did they think I was hanging around out of politeness after the breakup? Did they think I was waiting for another moment of weakness to jump her? Or could they accept that I was just someone to whom she had grown close in a necessary silence at the end of a relationship that had hurt her? I didn't know myself. It was easy to be there and let things happen. No drama. Just company. Familiarity.

I wondered if it would happen. I wondered if that was what we were building up toward. Physically we were more distant than when she had been with him, as if without him around, we didn't know where the boundaries lay. I hoped for something more, but then I didn't know, because when you get to the stage with someone where you don't have to think anymore, when you don't hear their voice as something outside yourself, then you miss it when it's gone. Any change in what was happening between us seemed like it could unbalance everything. I could live with this. There was a friendship that must have been getting deeper. It was better than what had been there before. But I still wanted her.

I saw his friend Patrick in a bank. I tried to look away, but he noticed me and stopped.

"Alex's friend," he said. "I've forgotten your name."

"Hello, Patrick," I said. "It's David."

"Right, yeah. How are you?"

"Fine. And you?"

"Great. Have you heard from the boy?"

"No, I haven't. Have you?"

"I spoke to him last week," he said. "In great form. Working on some Canadian film that's shooting near Versailles. Set up in a flat."

"Great."

"Meeting loads of people through Harry. Do you know Harry?"

"No."

"He was in first year with us. He's been there a while, so he knows loads of people. The two of them are running amok. He said they weren't, but Billy was talking to Harry, and apparently it's been very heavy. You can imagine."

"Sure."

"Are you planning on going over?"

"I'm not sure. With work and all."

"What do you do?"

"I'm in financial services. IT sort of stuff."

"Oh, right." He stood looking at me for a moment, trying to remember where he was and why he was talking to me. "Anyway. I better run," he said. "Good to see you. If you're talking to Alex, say hi. Tell him to give me a shout. I'm going to try and go in January."

"Okay."

I told Camille when I met her that night and we were walking into town. I didn't know whether it was the right thing to do, but not telling seemed like a big deal. I told her what Patrick had said, trying to be as accurate as I could, getting the phrases right, leaving my interpretation out of it.

"Sounds about right," she said.

"I thought so." I couldn't look at her to see what she was thinking as we walked.

After a moment she asked me, "Have you spoken to him?"

"Me? No. Why? Have you?"

"No. I rang him one time, but I didn't leave a message, and then he rang back, and he didn't either. Back and forth a couple of times, no message. And that was it."

"Nothing to say?"

"There's plenty to say. But I don't know . . ." I waited. We walked in silence for long enough that I thought we'd moved on. "I'll maybe see him over Christmas," she said then. "Find out how he's getting on."

"Right." I wanted to say something else to her. To ask her a question out of concern, to see if she was all right, but nothing came to me. It seemed like it wasn't my business. There were things I could have talked about myself. The pointless twinge of jealousy that I had felt hearing that he was having a good time, that he had found work, that things were going well. Of course I wanted him to be happy. But in some way I wanted him to struggle without me and the help and advice that I gave him. I was here, and I was with her. So what? What good was it? He would laugh if he saw the two of us clinging emotionally onto one another for support while he had moved on to the next phase of his life without looking back.

"Do you miss him?" she said.

"Sometimes. Yeah. Do you ever?"

"Not really. But then we weren't together for long. And the good times didn't last. It was only a couple of months, really. I know he's your friend," she said, "but he's an emotional fuckup."

"Yeah," I said. "I suppose so."

"But then look at us," she said, and I laughed because it seemed right.

It was as if we had both been holding our breath, afraid that the mention of his name would change something. I had thought that maybe if I talked about him, I would bring everything that had been left behind into the foreground again, as if she had forgotten him and it was within my power to keep his memory from her. As if his name was the word that would wake us from this dream and let us know that whatever had happened since then wasn't real. When you ask yourself, Is this a dream? it always is. You can hold on to it for a time,

keep moving forward, driving it further and further into un-
reality, but you know that it's over. You have to wake up.

We were in her house a few nights later, watching a film. At
the end, when she flicked it off, she stood in front of me at an
angle. There was something there, the way that she waited a
second too long without saying anything, that made me look
up. She held her hand out to me. I took it and stood up facing
her. There was nothing that I could say, as if the moment
would pop and be gone if I spoke.

"Come on," she said, and I went. Down the hallway and
into her room. We hesitated beside her bed, a moment of
nervousness.

"He's not here, is he?" I asked. "He's not going to jump out
of a cupboard and stab me or something?"

"No," she said. "He's gone."

We knew each other already. Everything else faded away
into the background. Work became a distraction. She stayed
at my place most of the time, and when I got home from work,
she would be there. I was with her.

But I still had to work at it. There were limits to what I
could tell her and what she would tell me. There were things
she didn't want to talk about and things I didn't want to
know. Comparisons. Personal histories. Versions of events
that would have to be edited, rewritten, excised. If she had
told me before that she missed Alex, I would have understood, but now? Was she allowed to? Was I? Our pasts would
keep changing to fit what was happening between us. Before,
when I had been imagining the two of us together, my fantasy
wasn't just about her. It was about me as well, as if by being

with her I would become somebody else. Somebody confident and fluent and certain. Somebody who knew what to do in any situation. But I was still the same person. I didn't change overnight just because I was with her. It made me think before speaking. She noticed it. This reticence. The hesitation before answering questions.

"Just talk to me," she said to me after a couple of weeks. "Speak. What's the problem? You should just say what you're feeling. Nobody will die."

"I don't know. I have to think."

"You think too much," she said.

"You've noticed that, then?" I said and laughed.

"Yes. Of course. Why?"

"I thought I was keeping it hidden."

"You can't hide things from me. I know everything now."

"And yet still you're here."

"I am still here," she said.

It was a couple of weeks before Christmas. I was going to meet her after work. The streets were packed in the center at seven o'clock on a Thursday night, the people moving in file and swelling at the crossing points until they spilled onto the road. It was still too early for the edge to have come into it, and the crowd moved together, docile and happy, the sound of footsteps and the music from shops and talking. I was letting myself be carried south to where I had to meet her. As we waited to cross from Westmoreland Street onto College Green, I saw Alex. He was straight across from me, and when the light changed, we would come face to face with each other. In the moment after I saw him, after the initial thrill that I couldn't deny, I thought about turning around and walking away up the street. It was like I'd been caught doing something, as if I owed him something that I'd lost. But then he saw me and smiled, and when the light changed and the blips pulsed, he stood still and I crossed toward him. I held out my hand when I arrived, and he shook it. He had lost weight. He was dressed differently in some way that I noticed but couldn't describe. He seemed taller, and as we spoke, he looked away from me, not meeting my eye. He was smiling still, but it wasn't at me.

"I didn't know you were back," I said.

"Monday, yeah. How are you?"

"I'm fine. And yourself?"

"Grand."

"So how's it going. How is Paris?" I asked.

"Wet. No. I don't know. It's great."

"You've settled in?"

"Yeah. More or less."

"I met your friend Patrick on the street. He'd heard you were having a great time."

"Trying to. How's your work?"

"It's fine. I'm still getting used to it." A moment of pause. "I didn't know you were back," I said again.

"Yeah, I was going to ring you. But you know what it's like when you come home."

"Yeah. Sure. What are you doing now?"

"Now? I'm meeting some friends for a drink."

"Right."

"And you?"

"Not much. Just going home."

There was nothing there. I knew I had to say something. I knew it would come out awkward before I said it, but there was nothing I could do.

"I'm seeing Camille now. I thought I should tell you. Or maybe you'd heard."

"I hadn't, no." He nodded and kind of smiled to himself. It could have meant anything. "Are you really? I'm glad," he said. "I hope it goes well for you. For you both."

"Thanks. It's good of you to say that." The words began to take shape. "Because I still feel shit about how it all ended. It wasn't right and I'm sorry and it's good to see you now. I've missed you around the place. So maybe we could meet up and try and sort it out. I'm sure Camille would want to see you too. How long are you home for?"

"Sunday."

"Sunday? You're not even staying for Christmas?"

"No. I've a job starting next week. This was all the time I could take."

"Okay," I said. "Well, maybe over the weekend?"

Now he looked at me.

"I don't know. It seems like a good place to leave it to me."

"Leave what?"

"If you're with her, then that's great for both of you. I'm sure you'll be very happy or whatever. You're both nice people. And I'm doing fine, it's all going well, and I'm getting work and that. So I don't know. I don't want to be dragging up a whole load of poisonous old shit that's only going to bring me down. Bring us all down. Because it would, you know. So I wish you well, really I do, but I better go on. Okay?"

"Okay," I said after a second. My head was reeling as if I'd been punched. He was so calm and unmoved that I couldn't square his words with the meaning. The idea wouldn't hold for me. He patted me on the shoulder quickly, smiled at me.

"No hard feelings," he said and crossed the road.

He disappeared into the flow of people heading north. I started walking on toward the pub and then stopped for a moment and turned. I tried to run through the crowd on the pavement, but it was impossible. I stepped out into the road and ran along looking for him. When I got as far as the bridge, I stopped. There were ten side streets he could have gone down. Roads in every direction. Taxis and buses and cars. He could be anywhere. I stood there and waited for a moment, hoping that the same instinct might bring him to me, but after a minute or two I realized that it was stupid, that he was just gone.

Acknowledgments

Thanks to Marianne Gunn O'Connor, Claire Wachtel, Cormac Kinsella, Andrew Ryan, Sarah Binchy, and my family.